WHEN YOU'RE SMILING

THE DI BENJAMIN KIDD THRILLERS
BOOK 1

GS RHODES

DARK SHIP CRIME

WHEN YOU'RE SMILING

To all those who told me to jump. Thank you.

ALSO BY GS RHODES

The DI Benjamin Kidd Thrillers

When You're Smiling

Just Keep Breathing

Your Best Shot

Be My Baby

Hand On Heart

Sticks and Stones

One Last Smile

Beyond The Sea

Exit Stage Death (Coming Soon)

The DS Zoe Sanchez Thrillers

Deadly Tears

Deadly Vengeance (Coming Soon)

CHAPTER
ONE

"You've absolutely got to see this! Trust me!" TJ was alight with excitement. He was practically bouncing from foot to foot, the mud squelching beneath his battered Converse, his face split in two by a smile so wild he looked like he was about to explode.

Lydia Coles sighed as a heavy wind blew through the park, almost knocking her sideways. The trees were leaning over, leaves were flying about in the breeze, and it was cold. So darn cold. She pulled her jacket tighter around her, tucked her hands into her sleeves, and stomped after TJ.

"But it's creepy out here," she complained, looking about. The further into the park they went the less clear the paths were, the more the trees seemed to encroach. And with the skies being dark grey and the weather being unpredictable, it was enough to freak her out more than a little bit. Every time a twig snapped she practically jumped out of her skin. "And it's cold!" she added quickly. TJ wasn't listening. He was way too excited about... well... about whatever the heck it was he wanted to show her.

If Lydia had known they were coming out this far, this late in the day, she might have dressed a little more appropriately. But when TJ appeared outside the lecture hall telling her he'd seen something that she *just had to see*, what could she say?

Well, she could have said no. But he was so excited, practically vibrating, smiling that same smile he had on his face now.

So, now she was traipsing through a park on the other side of town, not wearing a thick enough jacket for this time of year, and it looked like it was about to chuck it down.

She looked up to the sky and felt a drop hit her forehead.

Great, she thought. *That's just what I need. Rain. Christ.*

"TJ, can we just go back?" she groaned. She knew she sounded whiny, but she didn't care. Not right now anyhow. "I'm cold."

"We're almost there!"

TJ was up ahead, his baseball cap on backwards, his jeans hanging around his arse, wearing the biggest hoodie Lydia had ever seen. She remembered how in cartoons when people were hungry whoever they were with started to look like a delicious steak or something. Right now, TJ Bell looked like a radiator or a giant fluffy blanket she wanted to snuggle up next to. She didn't have feelings for TJ or anything, but she was seriously tempted to ask if she could either borrow his hoodie or climb in there with him.

She didn't see him agreeing to either.

They moved towards the trees, Lydia's boots squelching in the mud. She couldn't quite figure how far they'd come from the path, how far they'd even walked from TJ's car. Had she been here before? She couldn't be sure. But as they got closer and closer to a collection of dense trees, Lydia found herself feeling more and more unsure. Her heart started to pound a little harder in her chest. She didn't like this. She didn't like this one bit.

"TJ, please can we just go?" She trusted TJ. They'd been friends pretty much since they'd started uni, but to bring her out into the middle of nowhere when the weather was like this, when there was nobody else around… It made her suddenly feel suspicious. And she didn't want to be suspicious of a guy like TJ. He was meant to be one of the good ones.

"Almost there, chicken."

He slowed down, giving her a chance to catch up. They were stood next to one another by some densely packed trees, the smallest inlet just big enough for them to fit through one at a time, opening before them like the mouth of a beast. The scraggly, bare branches clawed out at them, reaching for the heavy, grey clouds above. All it needed was a thunder crack and the nightmare would be complete.

TJ looked down at Lydia.

"What?" she said.

"You ready?" He was grinning like a madman.

Good, that makes me feel calm, she thought, trying not to let her nerves show on her face.

"If this is lame, I'm not talking to you for the rest of the night." She couldn't keep the shake out of her voice. Was it the cold or was she really scared right now? She couldn't tell. Her heart was beating so fast it was practically humming.

TJ laughed, it was sort of like a bark, just a, 'HA!' that echoed off into the distance. It made her flinch. "Don't worry, Lyds, this is worth the trek."

She sighed as he set off again, entering the beast's mouth, leading the two of them slowly into the trees. It was darker in here. What limited light the sky was giving them was blocked out by the tree canopy.

Lydia cringed as she walked. She hated the feel of the damp foliage on her skin, of the sharp branches clawing at her like they were trying to grab hold and keep her there. Everything about it was claustrophobic. Who knew you could be out in the open and still feel like the walls were closing in?

They walked along a pathway that had been trodden down by people over the years, their shoes squelching, the fallen branches snapping underfoot. A chill ran through Lydia's body. She didn't know if it was anticipation or nerves.

"Here," TJ said finally, stopping dead in the middle of the path. Lydia couldn't see past him and, wondering what on earth they were supposed to be looking at, let out a heaving breath before stomping around him.

What met her eyes was a sight that she would never forget for as long as she lived.

There was a woman on the ground.

Or perhaps it was more accurate to say a woman's body.

She was pale, her hair covered in mud and dirt, wet from the rain. She was fully clothed, wearing a pair of jeans and a t-shirt that was drenched in blood and dirt and rain and plastered to her skin. But it was the face that made Lydia's breath catch in her chest.

The face was pretty messed up and barely recognizable as human. Carved into her cheeks were two crosses, the skin flapping open, pale red, some of the blood still present on her face. And across her neck was a deep wound like a smile. If you looked at it wrong, or maybe even right, it looked like a laughing face, and it was enough to make Lydia need to turn away. But each time she blinked there it was. She doubled over, trying to get some air into her lungs.

"What the fuck, TJ?" she breathed.

"I thought you'd want to see it," he said, totally nonplussed. She looked up at him. He was still staring at the body, not looking at her. How was he not repulsed by this? How was this not freaking him out?

"Why?"

He shrugged. "I saw it this morning."

"What were you doing in a forest this morning?"

"What are you, the police?" he parried, turning to look at her, suddenly on the defensive. Lydia would have taken a step back but the path was so small, the trees keeping them close together. Too close together at this point. "I was out for a run, and when I was done I wandered in here because it looked like a cool place to take photos and…" He nodded towards the body. It felt weird to be talking about her like she wasn't there. It felt rude, somehow. Though they could hardly include her.

"Did you call the police?" Lydia snapped.

"No, I thought you'd want to see it."

Lydia looked at him carefully. There was a question that ran through her mind and out the other side—did he know something about this?—but she shook the thought away as quickly as it came. There was no way. Was there?

He didn't seem any different. He was the same old happy-go-lucky, a little bit dumb but cute so who cared, TJ. He widened his eyes at her.

"Lydia, you don't think—?"

"Stop talking, TJ," she said suddenly. She didn't want to talk about it with him. Of course, he didn't know anything about this. How could he? It was TJ. There was no way. She shook the thought from her head, making a mental note not to bring it up with herself again.

She looked at the body one more time, at the way the knife had gone from under the woman's ear on either side, the way the wound bloomed as if it was a pair of lips opening. Messy, but effective. Clearly.

She took her phone out of her pocket, tapped it a few times, and pressed it to her ear, annoyed when she got a busy tone.

"Jesus," she groaned, tapping at the phone again to redial.

"Police?" TJ said.

"You call the police," Lydia said. "I have a friend who would die to see this too." She bit her lip and looked down at the body. "Sorry, bad choice of words."

CHAPTER
TWO

The blue lights shot past the pub window and Detective Inspector Benjamin Kidd almost knocked his pint over. He caught it just in time, grabbing it with a thick hand before he could spill a drop. He looked around to see if anyone had noticed. Everybody in the dimly lit pub was either focussed on Sky Sports News on the big TV screen or on drowning their sorrows. They weren't bothered about him. The only person who was bothered was Liz, sitting across from him, trying to stifle her laughter.

He always seemed to do that. Even before he was forced to take time off due to what DCI Weaver had called "stress" and "not taking a fucking break." Maybe it was instinct. Maybe it was obsession. He didn't want to say it was either.

"You're out of your mind," Liz finally said when she calmed down, wiping a tear from her eye. She was halfway down her third glass of white wine, her speech a little less than perfect, her smile getting lazier as the seconds passed by. She should have just bought the bottle.

Ben's sister, Elizabeth Spencer (formerly Kidd), was on what was one of her first nights out since her second baby was born, leaving little newborn, Timothy and three-year-old, Tilly with their father. "Do you always have to do that?" she asked, genuinely curious.

"Do what?"

"Sit bolt upright every time a police car goes past," she said, taking another sip. Her lipstick had already stained the rim of the glass. Kidd was surprised there was any left on her lips at all. "You're like a dog."

"Call the response Pavlovian."

"I'm not even going to pretend I know what that is," she replied with a lazy smile. "It's not healthy."

Kidd didn't know how to respond to that. He knew it wasn't healthy, but he'd done everything he thought he was supposed to do when he became a policeman some twenty-odd years ago. He'd thrown himself into it. He'd jumped at every opportunity, every scrap of overtime, and worked his way up to DI. Getting signed off with stress when, as far as he was concerned, he was just doing the job he wasn't paid nearly enough to do, sucked the big one. The last six months had been tough.

He took a sip of his drink.

"Is that agreement? Or are you hoping I'll change the subject?" Liz teased. Kidd smiled at her.

"How's Tiny Tim?"

"Oh, don't call him that, Ben, you know I hate that."

"That's why I do it," he replied, still smiling.

"You know, I hate you sometimes?"

Kidd shrugged. "No, you don't."

"No, you're right, I don't," she said. "I just worry about you, that's all." It was enough to stop Kidd from smiling, enough for him to put his drink down and look his sister square in the face. He didn't know what to say next, didn't know whether to thank her or tell her not to worry about him or— "Tim is fine," she said, interrupting his runaway freight train of a thought pattern.

"Huh?"

"Your nephew," Liz said. "He's doing well, settling in fine. He's crying a little bit too much at night for Greg's liking, but what can you do, eh? He's a baby. Babies cry."

"Is Greg crying too?"

"Don't start on Greg, Ben, not tonight." Liz groaned. "He likes you, you know. I don't understand why you're always such a dick to him."

Kidd laughed. "Oh Lizzy, I'm a dick to him because he makes it *far* too easy to be a dick to him," he replied. "He keeps setting them up, so I keep on knocking them down." Kidd took a sip of his drink and then sighed as he saw Liz looked a few shades more miserable than she had a second ago. "I'm totally kidding," he added. "Greg is great, you know that. He's a great dad; he's a great guy."

"I know that," she said. "I just want *you* to know that." She raised her eyebrows at him.

Kidd nodded. "You don't need to worry about me," Kidd said. "Really, you don't."

Liz eyed him carefully. She was the one person in his life who had known him the longest. Their parents aside, of course, Liz had been by his side for most of his good times and his bad, so she had this way of looking into him and seeing beyond the veneer he put up in the presence of other people. She could break through that barrier and pierce right into him, which meant she was listening to what he was saying and she wasn't buying a damn word of it.

"Okay, I'm going to tell you why I'm worried about you, and then you're going to tell me why I don't need to worry, alright?" she said, putting her nearly empty wine glass on the table in front of her. "And we'll see if you're in any way convincing because what you're selling right now, I'm not even close to buying."

"Liz—"

"If this is an auction, I'm not even bidding, I'm watching the other suckers interested in this shit, wondering what on earth they're thinking."

"Liz—"

"Don't worry, I'll make it quick," she said with a wink. "I'm worried because you don't seem to go anywhere or do anything."

"I run."

"That's exercise."

"That's doing something."

"But it's solitary, Ben, what about your friends?" His silence was telling. "You've spent most of your leave, what? Stressing about going back to work? Moping around the house? Looking for someone who maybe doesn't want to be found at this point or maybe can't be found?"

And those last words hit like a punch to the heart. It winded him in ways that he certainly wasn't prepared for. When he'd agreed to come out with Liz tonight, the plan had been to get a couple of drinks and talk about old times, maybe laugh about all the shit that went down at Christmas just last month, how he'd got so drunk at New Years that he was asleep at 10 pm in Tilly's room holding a stuffed toy.

Kidd wasn't prepared to dig around in a past that he'd tried to bury in work, in running as far as he could most mornings of the week, drowning it in a bottle of whiskey if it dared try to resurface.

The last person he wanted to think about was Craig Peyton.

Kidd could still see him as clear as day in his mind's eye. He was there most times he blinked, his blonde hair that was so long he always had to do this little hair flick to get it out of his face, blue eyes so sparkling that you couldn't look at them for all that long because it felt a bit too intense. Pouty lips. A scent all his own.

"See? I've lost you to him already," Liz said softly, reaching across the table and stroking Kidd's bare forearm. He yanked it off the table. "Sorry."

"Don't apologise," he said looking up, forcing a smile, though why he felt the need to try and convince

Liz that the thought of Craig didn't make him die inside, was beyond him.

Craig had been missing for nearly two years at this point. The worst part of it was that Kidd hadn't noticed at first. He thought Craig was being off with him, playing hard to get, despite the fact they'd been together for close to three years. Then his parents had got in touch wondering where he was. And Kidd's blood ran cold.

They never found him. Alive or dead.

To this day, Kidd had no idea where Craig had gone. He ignored every call, every text message, every email. He either ignored them, or he couldn't answer. Kidd had no idea. The police closed the case and Craig joined an ocean of people destined to never be found. It was enough to drive a person crazy.

"I shouldn't have said anything," Liz said. "But it worries me, Ben. I know you loved him." Kidd winced a little at the past tense. "I know that, but you can't keep waiting for the phone to ring. You can't keep waiting for your life to start again, because if you wait for it to start, you'll blink and the whole thing will have passed you by, you know? Maybe you need a hobby."

Kidd shrugged, taking a long swig of his drink, and then another, and then another until he could see the bottom of the glass. He let out a shaking breath.

"Do you want one more?" he asked, forcing his smile a little bigger.

Liz sighed. "If you're buying."

Kidd got to his feet and headed over to the bar. He

squeezed past a few people, edging around tables, and trying to ignore how sticky the floor was. At the bar, he caught sight of himself in the mirror and was struck by how similar he and Liz looked. The same light brown hair, their father's green eyes, their mother's full lips. They'd been mistaken for twins on more than one occasion, though Kidd was older, which always put Liz in a fantastic mood.

The bartender shuffled over to him, a sheen of sweat present on her forehead, her dark hair pulled back into a ponytail so severe it lifted her entire face. Kidd's mum would have called it a Croydon facelift.

"What can I get you?" There was a whine to her voice, the end of the sentence seeming to go on forever.

"Um—"

"Let me," someone interrupted to Kidd's right. He was tall, dark hair swept over into an effortless little quiff, eyes sparkling from the lamps positioned along the bartop.

"You don't have to," Kidd said firmly.

"No, really, I want to," the man said, reaching out a hand. "John."

Kidd sighed. This wasn't exactly a regular occurrence, it was just enough to knock him off balance. He didn't want to be rude, so he smiled and took it. "Ben," he said. "And it's really not necessary." He turned back to the bartender. "A pint of Aspalls and a large glass of your house white."

"Gotcha," the bartender said, turning to go get the drinks, the 'a' of the "Gotcha" lingering on like a drone.

"Just a gin and tonic for me please, darling," the man said, flashing her the most perfect set of teeth Kidd had ever seen. The bartender shrugged and walked away. She didn't care who was buying them, she was just wishing her shift was over. Kidd couldn't blame her. This might have been his local, but the place itself was pretty grim. Wall to wall middle-aged men who had no doubt been hitting on her since the second they walked in. At least it might not have been so bad as it was a Wednesday night. At a weekend it had to be a nightmare.

"Let me buy you and…" The guy, John, turned to the table Kidd had come from. So he had been watching him long enough to see where he'd come from. Interesting. "Your sister a drink."

"Is that a guess or a hope?"

"You're not wearing a wedding ring, so it can't be a wife," John said with a raise of his eyebrow.

"Oh, so you're a detective." The irony wasn't lost on Kidd.

"Hardly. Just trying my luck."

Kidd's drinks were placed in front of him. "I'll just pay for these please," Kidd said, before turning back to John. "Bad luck this time, I'm afraid," he added as he tapped his card on the reader. "Thanks all the same."

Kidd was about to grab his drinks when John stepped a little closer to him. Kidd found it equal parts annoying and endearing, this guy was making a huge play here, there was no doubt about it. Kidd was flattered. It almost felt mean to rebuff him again.

"Just take my card," he said, taking a card out of his pocket and handing it to Kidd. "It's got my number on it, my email, if you change your mind, just message me, okay?"

Kidd didn't want to say that he wouldn't. The guy was trying hard. So, he took a breath and took the card, putting it in his trouser pocket, making a mental note to throw it away when he got home.

John didn't want to take any more chances, so stepped away from Kidd, who took his drinks and walked back over to the table, trying to ignore his cheeks glowing a little. He put the drinks down and could already feel Liz's eyes burning holes into him.

"What?" he said when he sat down and took his first sip. The first sip was always the best, even when it was your fourth pint. "Stop staring at me."

"Was that man at the bar making a move on you?"

Kidd shrugged.

"Ben! What the hell?!"

"Keep your voice down," he hissed. "You're drawing attention to yourself."

"What did you say?"

"He wanted to buy me a drink and I politely declined," Kidd said, trying to give her a look that told her to drop it. "Nothing happened."

"You did *not* politely decline, you flirted first," Liz said. "I saw you. You think just because I'm married I can't see flirting happening right in front of my face?" She was practically screaming it and there were a couple of older men at the tables nearby looking over with absolute disgust radiating from their faces.

"Liz, I told him I wasn't interested," Kidd said. "He wanted to buy me a drink, well, both of us actually, but I declined and now here I am, can we change the subject?"

Liz opened her mouth to say something but quickly closed it.

Kid sighed. "What?"

"Nothing."

"Liz."

It was Liz's turn to sigh. "Just was going to say he could have been your hobby, that's all."

She descended into laughter and even Kidd couldn't keep himself from laughing with her. But there were still the thoughts of Craig sitting at the edges of Kidd's mind that even another drink couldn't take away. And as he wandered home later, long after the conversation had drifted away from such things, Kidd couldn't help but wonder if the only hobby he really had, was missing Craig.

How pathetic.

CHAPTER
THREE

K idd wandered his usual route home, stumbling a little as he walked the path up towards his house. He'd walked Liz home first, despite her complaining about the cold, and apologised profusely to Greg about how drunk she was. He didn't seem to mind. He'd seen her giving birth, seeing her shitfaced was hardly going to put him off.

He got the key in the door at the third attempt and stepped inside, welcomed by the slight chill in the air where the heating hadn't switched itself on and the usual silence that seemed to linger here.

Even with the sound of the traffic on the road outside, it still felt so incredibly quiet. The noises of the pub had long-stopped ringing in his ears and the silence now filling his head was more deafening than he ever thought possible.

He took a breath and shut the door behind him with

a thud, shutting out the last bit of sound, the last bit of streetlight.

He took his coat off and hung it by the door, wiping his shoes on the mat before kicking them off and putting them in their usual spot. He started to wonder if he should get a dog, someone to greet him when he walked in the door. It might make things feel a little less... lonely. A dog would be excited to see him. Though maybe in his line of work it would be cruel to get a dog. He'd have to pay somebody to come and walk it every day, especially if he was on lates. Maybe a cat.

He shook his head. Maybe nothing at all.

Kidd walked into the kitchen and poured himself a glass of water, downing it before refilling it once again. He took it upstairs to his bedroom where he placed it on his bedside table. He switched on the lamp and sat on his bed in the soft orange glow.

If anything were to happen to him and his colleagues walked in here looking for clues of the kind of life he lived, it would all be here, laid out like the perfect picture of a single man. There were clothes and underwear left on the floor that needed to be washed at least a week or so ago. There was a pile of plates by the door from breakfasts in bed gone by, toast mostly, occasionally scrambled eggs if he felt like treating himself.

He rolled his eyes at that.

In what universe is scrambled eggs a treat?

A stack of half-read books on his bedside table and the remnants of last night's water. At least the bed was made. That was something. They might be fooled into thinking that in the mornings he had his life together and, as the day passed by, he lost control little by little.

He stood back up and threw the clothes into the washing basket, before grabbing the plates from the chest of drawers by the door and running them downstairs and stacking them in the dishwasher. When he got back upstairs, the bedroom already looked better, less like a war zone.

He sighed and sat back on the bed, picking up his phone to see that it was barely 10 pm.

When did I become the kind of person who was in before 10 pm? he thought.

Then it started to ring in his hand, a horrible coincidence that almost made him instantly hang up. Until he saw who it was that was phoning him.

Patrick Weaver.

DCI Patrick Weaver.

For a moment that felt like it stretched into hours, Kidd stared at the ringing phone, the vibrations tickling his fingers. What on earth was DCI Weaver calling him for?

Whatever it was, he knew it couldn't be good.

With a heavy breath, Kidd answered. "Hello?"

"Kidd?" Weaver growled down the phone, a thick, Scottish baritone.

"Weaver," Kidd replied, brightening his voice perhaps a little too much. It was like he was trying to convince a parent he wasn't a little bit tipsy. "How are you?"

"Good, Kidd, good," Weaver said. There was something in the way he said *good* that Kidd didn't like, as if he was having to force the words out. "Is it a bad time?"

"No, not at all, sir," Kidd replied, standing up and starting to pace around his bedroom, thankful he wasn't having to kick clothes out of the way as he walked. "What can I do for you?"

"Um…" Weaver trailed off. Kidd knew he was still there because he could hear him breathing into the receiver. If he was struggling to even get the word out, then this couldn't be good at all. There was a shuffling of papers on the other end of the line.

10 pm and Weaver is still in the office, Kidd thought. The boss usually vanished as soon as the clock hit 5 pm, sometimes before if he could swing it. *This is not going to be good.*

Kidd took the initiative.

"It's a little late, isn't it?" Kidd offered, stifling a yawn almost to prove his point. "Is everything okay?"

Weaver sighed, the heavy breath distorting the line. "Not really."

"Oh."

"Aye," he rumbled down the phone. "I wouldn't normally do this, Kidd, you know I wouldn't."

"You're not exactly one for social calls, sir, I assumed it was going to be something work-related when I saw your name on the screen."

"Aye, right," Weaver said, taking another breath. "Are you sitting down?"

"No, but the longer you don't tell me what's happening, the more nervous you're making me," Kidd said, laughing a little. It was a half-truth, his heart rate was certainly up.

Weaver sighed again. "You're all set to come back in to work next week, aren't you?" he said.

"Yes," Kidd answered slowly. "Why?"

"I wouldn't ask, Kidd, you know I wouldn't," he said. "Not unless I thought it was necessary. And what's a few extra days, hmm?"

"Sir, with all due respect, I'm not totally sure what you're getting at here."

"Can you come in tomorrow?" Weaver blurted.

Kidd furrowed his brow, thankful that his boss wasn't here to see it.

"I suppose," Kidd said, suddenly regretting the fourth pint. He was going to look a bit of a state if his boss wanted a catch-up tomorrow. "What time?" he asked cautiously.

"Late morning will be fine," Weaver said. "Say eleven?"

"Alright then, boss, I'll meet you at the station at eleven," Kidd said.

The phone line was silent now. Kidd could hear Weaver shuffling about on the other end of the line. There was something else. There had to be something else, there was no way Weaver would be calling this late at night unless something—

"It's The Grinning Murders, Kidd," Weaver added suddenly. "We found a body a couple of days ago and… well… it looks mighty similar."

Kidd felt like the rug had been pulled out from beneath his feet.

"Kidd?" Weaver asked. "Kidd, are you still there?"

DI Benjamin Kidd's legs practically gave way beneath him as he sat down on the bed, the words running around in is head.

The Grinning Murders, he thought. *It's impossible.*

CHAPTER
FOUR

K idd could remember The Grinning Murders as
clear as day.

It had been fifteen years ago, but something like that
wasn't easy to forget, at least not in a hurry. It was one of
his early cases as a DC. He remembered people saying to
him when the body was found, "That'll put hairs on
your chest," and the like, but he hadn't imagined it
would follow him around for the rest of his career,
haunting him. Just the mention of it pulled up the
images in his head. The bodies of the victims lying face
up on the ground, crosses for eyes cut into their cheeks,
their necks splayed open like a big red smile. He'd seen
too many of them—three, though it was almost four—
before they'd managed to catch the guy.

Albert Hansen. Just thinking the name sent a shiver
down his spine.

They'd brought him in for questioning early on in the
case, dragging him out of the house in front of his son,

and he'd somehow managed to talk his way out of it. Imagine the shock to everyone on the team when the needle pointed back at Hansen and they realised he'd managed to pull the wool over their eyes.

When it came down to it, they only just managed to rescue the woman who was supposed to be his next victim.

"Kidd, you still there?" Weaver asked, a worried tone prevalent in his voice now. Of course, he was worried, that had been such a huge case for Kidd, everybody knew it. He'd been the one who'd helped to put two and two together and come up with Hansen. He was the one that had found Hansen about to kill the fourth victim, the one who had chased him and tackled him to the ground. His name was all over it. The two things practically went hand in hand. Kidd and The Grinning Murders. A match made in hell.

"Still here, sir," Kidd managed, though his voice sounded a little less bright now. He needed a drink. Water. His mouth suddenly a desert. He grabbed the cup from his bedside table and downed half of it in one go. He took a breath before he spoke again. He needed details. He didn't want them, but if Weaver was bringing this up with him then he wanted Kidd involved. "When?"

"What's that?"

"When did you find a body?" he asked, trying to keep his voice calm even as the phone shook in his hand.

"Three days ago," he said. "Got called in by a couple

of university students who stumbled upon it in Bushy Park."

"Bushy Park, Jesus Christ." Kidd sighed. That wasn't even that far from where he was now, not in the grand scheme. If he walked through town and out the other side he would be there.

"My thoughts exactly," Weaver replied.

"But Hansen is in prison, isn't he?" Kidd said. Surely if someone like that had been let out early for good behaviour the media would have had a field day.

"Still there," Weaver said, flatly. "Like you said, I don't normally do social calls and I'm sure you've been coping fine on leave and this probably wasn't what you were expecting to come back to."

A case that was closed fifteen years ago? Kidd thought. *Certainly not.*

"But there isn't anyone who knows the case like you do, Kidd," Weaver said. "At least not someone who's still on the job. So, if you wouldn't mind—"

"I'll be there," Kidd interrupted. "Eleven still work for you?"

"Perfect," Weaver said. "I'll see you tomorrow."

"See you tomorrow, sir."

"And Kidd," Weaver said quickly. "Try and get some sleep tonight, eh? It's going to be a long one tomorrow, I imagine."

Kidd swallowed. He was used to the long hours, he'd done more than his fair share of eighteen-hour shifts since he joined the Met, but if there was someone out there copycatting Albert Hansen, all-nighters weren't off the cards. "Yes, sir."

Weaver hung up and Kidd sunk back down onto the bed, staring at the phone in his hand. Had that even just happened? The Grinning Murders had been so long ago. Sure, every now and again he would remember the bodies, remember Hansen, but he'd never thought it would happen again. Not like this. It made it even worse to think that it wasn't even Hansen doing it this time around, some nutcase, some fanatic. Weaver had told him to get to some sleep, but how was he supposed to sleep after all that?

After everything they'd gone through trying to get to the bottom of it the first time around…

The media had an absolute field day, a serial killer in a Royal Borough, like crime didn't exist if it wasn't somewhere in Central London. Between having to deal with the vultures writing their think pieces on how terrible the police were and actually having to catch the killer, Kidd was run off his feet, the whole team had been. It was enough to have all of them signed off with stress by the end, but they'd just gone back to work, business as usual. The newspapers had forgotten about it a few days later, like they hadn't just saved a woman's life.

But that was how it always seemed to be. The media would hound the police about what it was they were doing wrong, criticise and harass until they made the Commissioner come out with a statement. Then, the case would be solved and someone would be a hero for five minutes before they moved on to the next thing to complain about, the next police officer caught doing something wrong.

Kidd shook his head and put his phone on the bedside table. He went and brushed his teeth, trying to wind down, trying to push thoughts of the case out of his mind, but it didn't work. Every time he blinked he could see Albert Hansen's face, clear as a bell.

The dark curls, the clean-shaven face, the eyes such a dark shade of brown he almost looked like a shark. He was charming. That was the thing that surprised people the most when it got to the interview, when he ended up in the docks, he was incredibly charming. He was silver-tongued. It was the scariest thing about him. It wasn't just that he'd killed these people in such a brutal fashion, it was that he showed no remorse, it was that he was almost proud he'd gotten away with it for so long. When he was an early suspect so many people had said it couldn't possibly be him—he was so kind, so mild-mannered, so normal.

Kidd shook his head and spit out the toothpaste.

Being in the Met had changed him. It showed him the best and the worst of humanity on a daily basis. It taught him that anybody could be a killer. Absolutely anybody.

He looked at himself in the mirror. Maybe even he could be, under the right circumstances. You never knew what was going on in someone's head just by looking at them.

Kidd climbed into bed and turned off the light,

allowing himself to drown in the dark, in the quiet of it all. But sleep eluded him. Even with his eyes closed, his breathing deep, his brain ran a hundred miles an hour as it went through the case in minute detail.

Weaver had said tomorrow was going to be a long day, but it looked like tonight was going to be a long night too.

CHAPTER
FIVE

Kidd woke the following morning with light streaming through his bedroom window. He'd forgotten to shut the curtains, so the early morning sun had assaulted his eyelids instead of his alarm assaulting his ears, but waking naturally did little to improve his sour, sleep-deprived mood. He felt his age in his creaking bones as he sat up in bed.

The house was quiet, as it was most mornings, but for the sound of the traffic outside his window. It was fine most of the time, quietening down enough at night so he could sleep. Though, every now and again he would be awoken by a siren or by someone thinking that his road was the track at Silverstone.

He stayed in bed for a while longer than he normally would, knowing he had time to spare, knowing that once he got out of bed and committed to the day, he would be on the case.

The Grinning Murders, he thought. Even in the cold

light of the morning it still felt impossible, like he'd imagined it. How could it be real?

Even as he got himself ready, thoughts of that case echoed in the deepest recesses of his mind. He could still see the images of those dead bodies, of the cuts inflicted onto their faces. He could even see the look on Hansen's face when they'd finally caught him, one that was resigned to his fate. Maybe he'd known they were coming but simply couldn't stop himself. It was hard to tell.

He got changed into the same smart trousers he'd been wearing the previous night, a clean white shirt, tie and jacket. He threw his coat on and checked himself one last time in the mirror before he left. Was this the face of a man who was ready to step back into this life?

Kidd didn't want to dwell on the question for too long.

He decided to walk to work. He lived a little way away from Kingston Police Station and, even though it was probably far enough away to warrant driving, he felt he needed the walk to psyche himself up.

The morning was bright and cold, January in every sense of the word. The sun was doing its best to break through the haze and warm the world up, but was failing miserably, so Kidd pulled his jacket tightly around himself as he started to work.

He walked through town, past the shopping centre and the early morning hustle and bustle of people heading to their jobs, to college, to uni, and towards the riverside. Even though it had been covered in restaurants with a river view, the riverside was one of his favourite places in town, and at this time of the morning, it was basically dead. There was something about the water that calmed him. His parents had taken them to the seaside a lot when they were younger. He wondered if it was that. He associated the water with relaxation.

He stopped at the railing and looked out across the water, a team of rowers heading in one direction, the river cruise to Richmond heading in the other. He breathed in the cold morning air, like that would go some way to mentally preparing himself for what lay ahead.

Nope, he thought. No such luck.

His phone buzzed in his pocket, showing a message from Liz.

My head feels like it's been flattened by a steam roller. If you've gone running this morning I'm disowning you.

LOL, not even sorry. You brought it on yourself. Not out running, but I am already out. Lazy.

Why?

Seriously WHY?!

Work called. I'm heading back in.

Not wanting to hear Liz's complaints about him heading back into work before the end of his leave, Kidd flicked his phone to silent and pocketed it, heading away from the water.

When he reached the station, even from a distance, he recognized Weaver waiting outside holding a travel mug of coffee. He was tall, broad-shouldered, his ginger hair cut and styled neatly. He was built like a rugby player, the seams of his suit screaming where he stood. Like he could sense Kidd's eyes on him, Weaver turned as he approached, his face shifting to an awkward smile.

Kidd smiled back, though it was hard to ignore the fact that his boss had decided to meet him outside the office on his first day back. For some reason, that didn't sit well with Kidd, though he couldn't quite place why.

"Morning, boss," Kidd said once he was in hearing distance.

Weaver took a sip of his drink, probably wishing it was gin, before answering. "Morning, Kidd. Sleep well?"

"Terribly."

"How was leave?"

"Do you really want to know?"

Weaver gave him a tight-lipped smile before reaching out a hand for Kidd to shake. He took it. "We've missed you around here."

Kidd didn't know if the feeling was mutual. What he missed was feeling productive, feeling like he was actually doing something. It wasn't the same thing.

"Likewise," he lied, shaking Weaver's hand. "Shall we?"

Weaver took a breath. "Best get started, eh?"

Weaver headed inside and held the door open for Kidd. It still smelled the same, like someone had poured bleach over the entire reception area to give it the impression of being clean, even though it certainly wasn't.

"Well, as I live and breathe!" came a voice from behind the counter. Diane was the Station Reception Officer at Kingston Police Station and had worked there for longer than Kidd had. She was a staple, the kindest woman you could hope to meet. She knew everything, pretty much, and she was always there to look out for the people in the station. Her face burst into a smile when she saw him, like a family member you've not seen since Christmas. It was nice to feel wanted upon his return, that much was for sure. "I wasn't expecting I'd ever see you again, Kidd," she added.

"Try and keep me away," Kidd deadpanned with a wink.

"How was leave?"

"Terrible," he said. "I couldn't stop thinking about you. I nearly came in here two or three times just to say hello."

"You know you would have been more than welcome. I could have fixed you a cup of tea, or got you a sandwich, you're getting thin," Diane replied, her cheeks flushing a little. "You come out here and talk to me later," she added. "I want to hear about everything you got up to over the past six months."

Kidd smiled. He didn't know quite how long it

would take to tell her that he ran a lot, read a lot, and generally avoided human contact for six months. But Diane was a good egg.

Weaver used his key card to open the door by the desk, the familiar bleep and sound of the metal magnets letting the door go were so familiar to Kidd it took him a moment to register they were happening in real life. He followed Weaver through the familiar hallways that he'd walked practically every day for the past twenty years. And now that he was coming back to them it felt like he'd been away for six years, not six months.

Noticeboards had changed. The doors looked like they were a different colour but probably weren't. The walls looked like they'd had a fresh coat of ugly beige paint, though they definitely hadn't.

Kidd breathed it in. It still smelled the same. He couldn't describe what the smell was exactly, only that he knew it would follow him around for the rest of his life.

Weaver took him straight through to his office, not what Kidd had been expecting. At least, that explained why he'd been waiting outside for him rather than letting him come in of his own accord.

"I'm sorry to bring you back before your leave was over," Weaver said as Kidd closed the door. "I wouldn't normally, but things are... well... you know what they are, you've been here, you've done this before."

"Something like that, yes," Kidd said, looking around the office. Even Weaver's office looked different than it had the last time he was here. It was cleaner. The usual chaotic desk looked like it had been tidied. He felt like he was losing his mind. "You change this office?"

Weaver eyed him carefully. "No. I don't think so anyway."

"It looks different," Kidd said. "You didn't tidy it on my account, did you?"

"Certainly not," Weaver replied, looking around, suddenly feeling self-conscious. "I've always been tidy, you must be misremembering. It's been six months."

"I know," Kidd replied, shaking the thought from his head and taking a seat across from Weaver. "So, what are we working with here?"

Weaver was still fixing him with a curious stare. "Are you sure you're up for this?"

"You're the one who brought me back."

"I know, I know, I just don't want you doing anything until you're ready," he said. "How are things in… in your personal life?"

Kidd sighed, already tired of this. "Shit, Weaver, things are shit, but doing this would go a heck of a long way to taking my mind off it."

They stared at each other across the table, a standoff bathed in the mid-morning sunlight coming through the cheap blinds.

Weaver sighed and reached for the file on his desk.

Kidd 1, Weaver 0.

He opened it and took out a couple of photos, placing them in front of Kidd. Inadvertently, he took a deep breath before looking down to see exactly what it was he was dealing with.

Still, it took him by surprise.

Even with the knowledge of it all, the memories of the original case burned into his memory, the pictures were still enough to knock the breath right out of him.

The first photograph was from a distance. There was a woman lying on the ground, face-up, obscured by mud and pretty banged up, blood covering her t-shirt, though clearly it had been raining because it wasn't the usual, deep-red colour. It had since faded to pink on the white fabric. Like she'd spilt red wine across her chest. The second photo was a little more close-up.

Carved into the woman's cheeks were the two crosses, like a pair of eyes, haphazardly hacked into her face. Then, there was the wound along the throat, that long curve, that sickening smile that haunted his dreams.

The woman's eyes were closed, thank heavens, but her hair was matted either with mud or blood. Kidd couldn't tell which. He didn't want to know.

"You see?" Weaver said. "It's the same, isn't it?"

"Somewhat," Kidd said, looking a little closer. He picked up the photo and leant back in his chair, running his eyes across it one more time, picking up on every detail, not just on the woman's body, but around it. He could see some blood stains beside her, marking the ground with spots of red like rain. "This was done at the location," Kidd said.

"Yes," Weaver replied.

"The others weren't," Kidd said flatly. "I don't remember them being anyway," he added, doubting his memory for a second. "If I remember it correctly, the bodies were normally, for want of a better word, dumped. This looks like it's been done there. It's a small thing, but it makes it different."

"That's why I asked you to come back in, Kidd," Weaver said, shaking his head. "It's something we would have come to eventually, I'm sure, only it would have taken a bit of looking for us to see that, but you noticed it straight away. You know this case like the back of your hand, and if we're going to catch the bastard doing this, we need all the help we can get."

Kidd sighed. "I just have one question," Kidd said, knowing he was repeating himself. "Hansen is definitely still in prison, right?"

Weaver nodded. "Locked up tight. He's not going anywhere."

"Right," Kidd said, turning his gaze back to the pictures. In some ways, it eased his mind to know that Hansen was in prison, that he wasn't the one who was a threat to anybody. But that just meant that they were looking for somebody else, somebody new, somebody who wouldn't have the same movements as Hansen. In a way, it made it harder. It could be anyone.

Kidd looked up at Weaver. "We'd best get started then, eh?"

CHAPTER
SIX

Weaver took Kidd down a labyrinth of familiar corridors to the Incident Room. It was one he'd worked in before. Thankfully, though, not the same one they'd used the last time he'd faced The Grinning Murders. That would have been a little too much.

When Weaver opened the door and walked inside four sets of eyes looked up sharply from where they were, like rabbits in headlights. There were only a couple of faces in that room that Kidd didn't know, that he hadn't worked with before, and somehow that made him more nervous than he would have been had he walked into a room full of strangers.

"Morning team," Weaver said, stepping inside and ushering Kidd in after him. He turned to Kidd. "Do I need to do introductions or would that be weird?"

"Probably be a little bit weird, sir," Kidd said, a smile tugging at the corners of his mouth. "But if you'd prefer—"

"Right then," Weaver said, stepping further into the room, clapping his hands and rubbing them together. He was in his element now, apparently pleased that he had something to do. He approached a desk, a young lad sat behind it pouring through what looked like old files from the previous case.

At least he's already doing his homework, Kidd thought.

"This is DC Simon Powell, don't believe you've met him before," Weaver said, gesturing to a young, heavyset boy in an ill-fitting blue suit. "Good lad, hard worker, sure he'll be an asset to the investigation."

"Thank you, sir," Simon said, a slight flush of pink coming to his chubby cheeks. His shirt was buttoned right to his neck, the knot of his tie small and tight. A pair of brown eyes looked out from a ghostly pale face. He stood up to greet Kidd, knocking some papers over, and a few empty paper cups from his desk. "Sorry… uh…" He scrambled to pick them up.

Kidd turned to Weaver and widened his eyes. If this lad was meant to be an asset, he dreaded to think what the future of policing looked like.

DC Powell stood up and smiled at Kidd, his cheeks still flushed. "Pleasure to meet you…" he trailed off, waiting for Kidd to say his name. Weaver got in ahead of him, enjoying being able to play host.

"This is DI Benjamin Kidd," Weaver said. "He's going to be SIO on this investigation. He—"

"You did it last time," Simon interrupted. Weaver cleared his throat. "Sorry, sir." He turned back to Kidd.

"Your name is all over these case files. You caught Albert Hansen."

"The team caught Albert Hansen," Kidd corrected, though he was certainly flattered. "But thanks. You keep looking over those case files, we need to get an evidence board started. You done one of those before?"

"No, sir."

Kidd tried not to sigh. *Give me strength,* he thought.

"Find someone who has, have them show you how to do it and get one going. I want to be able to see everything from the previous investigation and this one, make the connections, figure out what's going on."

"Yes, sir."

"You're going to frighten the kid off," a voice said from behind Kidd. He turned to see DC Owen Campbell, blonde hair shaved close to his head. He'd been working on his tan since Kidd last saw him and was offering Kidd a smile that was just as fake. "Come on, Si, I'll give you a hand."

Simon got to his feet and hurried to Owen's side like a lost puppy, eager to learn, eager to be liked, eager to do well. Kidd remembered being like that when he'd first joined the force. It was sweet.

"Didn't think we'd be seeing your face back here anytime soon, sir," Owen said with a wink. "Half expected you to vanish to an island somewhere and never return."

"Can't get rid of me that easy."

"Shame." Owen laughed. "Come on, Si."

Owen took Simon to the front of the room, the stack of case files in Simon's hands. Kidd watched him nearly drop them all, wincing as he crashed into the corner of a desk. He was going to have his hands full with that one, that much he could tell. Keen as anything but clumsy as heck. A killer combination. The two of them started talking in hushed tones. At least with Owen helping him, the board would have some order to it. Owen was good like that.

"This is DC Janya Ravel," Weaver said, taking Kidd over to another desk where an Asian woman sat working on her computer, her gaze held firmly on that screen until Weaver had spoken. She looked up sharply and fixed Kidd with a stiff, nervous-looking smile.

"Lovely to meet you," Kidd said, smiling back, wanting her to feel more at ease. Her black hair was pulled up into a rather conservative bun, her eyes big and wide as they stared up at him from where she sat.

"Lovely to meet you too," she said, letting out a breath, her smile looking a little less pained than it had a moment ago.

"And I don't need to introduce you to DS Sanchez."

"I should think not." DS Sanchez was sat over to one side of the room on a sofa, a disposable coffee cup in one hand, her phone in the other. Her dark brown curls had been pulled up and away from her face, a couple of strands hanging forward in front of her bright amber eyes. She raised an eyebrow at Kidd. "Hey, stranger."

"Morning, Zoe," Kidd said. "How's things?"

"We've got a murderer on the borough copying one of your old mates, how do you think things are?" she snapped, rolling her eyes, and turning her gaze back to her phone. DC Ravel flinched. So did Kidd. Things were definitely not good.

"I trust you know where everything is," Weaver said with a smile. "You hop to it. You know where to find me if you need me."

Kidd resisted the urge to say, "Pretending nothing is going on and staying out of the way." Instead, he smiled and said, "Thank you, sir." He might as well start off toeing the line. He could find a hundred or so ways to piss off Weaver without even thinking about it, best not start with one on his first day back.

Weaver left the Incident Room and Kidd turned his attention back to Zoe. Her eyes were fixed on him. She got up from the sofa and walked over, nodding for him to follow her. He did this gladly.

They walked over to a desk that Kidd could tell even from a distance was hers. It was messy, more than messy, it was chaos personified. There were papers stacked up one side, threatening to topple and fall to the ground, and more disposable coffee cups than was necessary.

She must never sleep, he thought.

"Wasn't expecting you back so soon," Zoe said as they got to her desk.

"No, me neither," Kidd said. "Do you own a travel mug, Zoe?"

"Excuse me?"

"A travel mug," Kidd said. "Might stop you from using all the disposables. Environment and all that."

She raised an eyebrow at him. "Really? You go off-grid for six months and the first thing you're talking to me about when you reappear is that I need to become an eco-warrior?"

"Not a warrior," Kidd said. "I just thought—"

"I messaged you," she said. "I called you. I even thought about coming to your house but I didn't want to intrude." She held his gaze, waiting for him to say something. When he didn't, she sighed and continued. "Where did you go?"

"Took a holiday," Kidd said.

"For six months?"

"No," Kidd replied. "For part of it, the rest of it I…" he trailed off. What had he been doing for the past six months? He'd read a lot, he'd run a lot, he'd watched more TV than was humanly possible. He'd done everything he could to purge the job from his mind. They signed him off with stress, their intention probably for him to *de*stress, to come back a changed man, but he spent most of it worrying there wouldn't be a job to come back to, that everything would have moved on without him.

He'd wanted to forget this place while he was off. And that had meant cutting himself off, but Zoe didn't see it like that.

"I know you, Ben," Zoe said, lowering her voice so as not to pull focus from the other DC's in the room. Ben looked around to see that Owen and Simon were busy working on the evidence board, DC Ravel had gone over to join them with some papers of her own. "You don't do a disappearing act for no good reason."

Kidd sighed. "If you know me, then you know that the only way I could be less stressed so I could come back would be if I disconnected," he said. "Anything else wouldn't work. And de-stressing was the whole idea, wasn't it?"

"And did it work?"

Kidd snorted. "What do you think?"

That got him a tight-lipped smile. A smile with a twinkle in her eye that meant that their friendship wasn't completely over.

"Boss?" Owen called from across the room. "We're about ready to get going over here, if you are."

"Thank God you're here, he's been acting like he's second in command all morning," Zoe grumbled.

"Really?"

"There was about to be a double murder."

Kidd snorted. "There's not a court in the world that would convict you."

"For killing Campbell?" Zoe smirked. "They'd give me a bloody medal. There'd be a statue of me in Market Square."

"Boss?" Campbell repeated.

Kidd and Zoe looked over towards the board where DC Powell and DC Ravel were also stood, their eyes trained on Kidd.

They turned back to each other. Zoe raised her

eyebrows at Kidd. "You ready, 'Boss'?" she said, her tone so loaded, it was practically a cocked gun.

Kidd smiled and took a deep breath, lowering his voice so the rest of the team wouldn't hear him. "Not even a little bit."

CHAPTER
SEVEN

Kidd walked to the front of the room, DS Sanchez close behind him. Owen and DC Powell got themselves out of the way so Kidd could get a decent look at the board. It was enough to turn even the hardiest officer's stomach.

Powell had put everything from the original case over to one side and Kidd stopped dead, staring at them wide-eyed like he'd seen a ghost. Because he had. Three ghosts, to be exact. Natalie Anders, the first victim, Angela Berry, the second, Karen Nicks, the third.

Once the third victim had been found, the media swooped in like a kettle of vultures. Nobody could stop the think pieces, the front pages, the aggressive hounding of the victims' families. Once you hit the third victim in a case, it becomes a serial killer, and there are few things the British public like more than the story of a sick serial killer out on the streets. There's an obsession with serial killers for a reason. People marvel at the mind of someone who can do something like that, who can be so cruel, so vicious, without any remorse.

Though, who was Kidd to judge. He'd dedicated his life to it.

The cuts in the cheeks, the slice through the neck, each one of them the same, methodical, careful, so clean it made it infuriating. The killer left nothing behind. Not a trace. With every body they found, they had practically nothing new to go on.

It had started as a code for him at first, calling them The Grinning Murders, but then the newspapers got hold of it and they ran with it. You couldn't move for it in the headlines. Every day they would speculate, stir up fear, trouble, just like they always did, even now. But in an age of social media, it all moved a heck of a lot quicker. You couldn't breathe without it being caught on camera and every faceless profile had an opinion.

Kidd had to stop paying attention to the newspapers. It was enough to drive him insane.

He looked across to the fourth picture. It was the picture that Weaver had shown him this morning, the one of the woman face up on the ground, covered in blood. Seeing them all next to each other, it didn't take a genius to see that this was different than the others. The women in the previous killings had all been completely clean but for the fatal wound to the neck and the gouges on their faces. Whoever this woman was, she'd been through it in a much worse way. Nothing about it was clean and precise. Everything pointed to someone trying to do it in a hurry.

Kidd turned to his team. "So, what do we have so far?"

Owen took a breath. "Waiting on a DNA match for the victim," he started. "We want to establish who she is, see if there's a connection to Hansen and the previous murders. Once we have that, we'll be able to figure out if there are any patterns, protect anybody who might be... in trouble." The hesitation made Kidd nervous. The fact that someone else could be in trouble made him *very* nervous. No time for that.

"Good start," he said. "What else?"

"Photographs have been taken, as you can see, forensics is looking for fingerprints, hair, fibres, anything that could point us in the direction of the killer," he continued.

"If they're really taking hints off Hansen, they wouldn't have left a single thing," Kidd said, stepping a little closer to the photo. "But I get the impression he's singing from the same hymn sheet but in a slightly different key."

"You think he's not as careful?" Zoe asked.

Kidd took a breath. "Honestly? I'm counting on it. Any connection with the locations of where the original bodies were found?" Kidd asked.

"Not that we can tell," Owen said.

"And time of death?"

Owen shrugged. "Going to have to wait for pathology on that one, sir."

Kidd knew that they needed to get that timeline as quickly as possible. If whoever was doing this was truly trying to replicate Hansen, they only had a few days before another body would show up. It was another place his efficiency had come into play. It had all happened in such quick succession, by the time they'd found one body and got any details from pathology another body had shown up. Nine days. Three bodies. How long could they possibly have here?

"Anything else, boss?" Owen asked.

"Who found the body?" Kidd asked, turning away from the board. "Weaver mentioned a couple of kids at the scene."

"Uni students," Zoe chimed in, the eye roll prevalent enough in her voice that Kidd didn't have to see it to know it was there. "They were walking through the woods in Bushy Park and found the body."

Kidd eyed her carefully. "Do you buy that?"

"All purchases were not final," Zoe said. "We've taken DNA from them, photographs of the shoes they were wearing for footprints to count them out of any investigation."

"They been questioned?"

Zoe shook her head. "They gave detailed statements. They're yet to be questioned by police."

"How are they?"

"Seemed a little rattled," Zoe said with a shrug. "But that's pretty understandable. It's one thing to find a body period, a whole other thing to find a body in this state." She sighed. "Sorry, DC Campbell, you want to carry on?"

Owen nodded. "Thank you, DS Sanchez," he said

turning back to the board triumphantly before turning back to face Kidd. "I… uh… I think that's all we have for now."

"Media?"

"We have a couple of news outlets picking it up," DC Ravel started. She was visibly shaking. "Some short articles already being written, some tweets here and there, but they don't have enough details to pin it to anything, least of all to Hansen. There are a few people putting two and two together, harassing us for more information, dropping Hansen's name, but all they really know is a body was found in Bushy Park, everything else is up for grabs."

"Good work," Kidd said. "Can you keep an eye on that? I don't want it to get out of hand if we can help it."

DC Ravel smiled. "Sure thing, sir." A smile was a good thing.

"Press conference?" Kidd asked the room.

"Weaver wants one arranged as soon as we have some leads," Owen said. "In an ideal world, I think he'd like it to be over and done with as quickly as possible because… well… it's The Grinning Murders." Just mentioning it out loud brought a strange hush to the room, even Campbell lowered his voice. "No one wants that media circus again."

Kidd nodded and looked up at the wall. It was like his past had come back to haunt his future. The irony of being signed off for stress and then brought back into the fold with something like this. It was enough to make him want to disappear to a desert island and not come back.

"Anything to add, sir?" Owen said.

Kidd walked over to the board and pointed at the newest picture. "It will be easier for us to put together a picture of what's going on when we know who the victim is," he started. "But there are already a few things I can see here that don't quite add up."

Zoe eyed him curiously like she was about to chime in, but Kidd carried on anyhow.

"She's lying in her own blood for a start," Kidd said bluntly. "If you look at the previous murders, or the case files of those murders, those bodies were dumped, they were never murdered at the scene. So that already makes one difference," he added. "And we know for a fact that it isn't Hansen."

"Why's that, sir?" Owen asked.

"Hansen is in prison," Kidd said. "He's serving three life sentences, he hasn't been let out and hopefully he never will be. This is a copycat. A shit copycat as well, if you ask me."

Kidd stared up at the board. He had that feeling of being watched. He knew the eyes of the team were on him. He needed to get started, get back into the swing of things. And he knew just where he wanted to start.

CHAPTER
EIGHT

Kidd headed out of the station, DS Sanchez in tow. He'd left the team to keep doing what they were doing, going through the case files, figuring out connections, finding leads, waiting for information from the lab, but he needed to get out. When it came to the start of an investigation, Kidd always liked to start at the scene of the crime. It's just what made sense to him.

"You don't need to see it, you know?" Zoe said. "We've got the pictures, we've had officers there, we've got statements."

Kidd shook his head. "I need to be there," he replied. "Maybe it's old fashioned but I want to start at the very beginning."

"I've heard it's a very good place to start," Zoe said as she followed him out of the building and into the car park. "You want to drive, or shall I?"

"You're more than welcome," he said, heading towards an electric blue Focus, one of the unmarked police cars in the car park, pulling his jacket tight as the wind whipped about him.

"Good," Zoe said with a smirk. "You're a shit driver. I hate being your passenger."

Kidd looked at her carefully, his eyebrow arched, a laugh bubbling beneath the surface. He laughed as he hopped into the passenger seat.

"What are you laughing at?" Zoe asked as she got in, pulling on her seatbelt.

"It's taken you literally fifteen minutes before you started ripping into me again," Kidd said. "Some things never change."

And Kidd was sort of glad of that. Zoe hadn't exactly seemed pleased to see him when he'd walked into the station. He thought there was going to be some tension between them but they seemed to be picking up where they'd left off. The last thing he wanted was for their relationship to be damaged, or for him to be treated differently because he'd been signed off.

"Well," Zoe started, switching on the engine. "Any excuse to remind you that you shouldn't be allowed to drive." She turned to him. "You ready for this?"

"For what? Are you about to start doing doughnuts in the car park or something?"

Zoe snorted. "No, I mean to be back at a crime scene. It's been a while, Kidd."

Kidd sighed, this was what he'd been afraid of. "I don't need to be babied, Zoe. The sooner we get this investigation started, the sooner we get our killer."

"The body is already with the pathologist."

"Don't want to see the body," Kidd said, knowing that it was yet another image that would stay fixed in his mind for the rest of his life. "I want to see where it happened. I want to be able to trace the killer's steps. It helps. Trust me."

Zoe shrugged. "You're yet to give me a reason to doubt you."

She pulled out of the car park and started them away from Kingston towards Bushy Park. He still couldn't believe it was in Bushy Park. How on earth had the killer managed to get a woman into the trees at Bushy Park and kill her without being seen? Or even heard? It didn't make sense.

Kidd shook his head. This person wasn't as careful as Hansen had been all those years ago. They were more focussed on replicating the method, not replicating the process. Everything about Hansen's killings had been careful, methodical, he'd known exactly what he was doing. It was what made it all the more terrifying. The bodies appeared and there wasn't any trace of how they got there, or how they were killed. This was messy. They were already making mistakes. At least, Kidd hoped they were. If they made mistakes it would be easier to track them down.

The roads were pretty clear given the time of day, so it wasn't long before they pulled into the car park and got out of the car. There were a couple of other police cars here, poor PCs that had no doubt been asked to stand at a cordon and answer any questions put to them by the nosiest members of the public, come rain or come shine. Kidd didn't envy them. He'd had to do it many times in his career and he would hate to go back to it. Now that people had mobile phones and they could record your every reaction? Absolutely not.

"Okay, so don't kill me for asking you this," Zoe started.

"Your choice of words isn't exactly great given the circumstances, but go on," Kidd said with a smile.

"Shit, yeah, sorry." Zoe shook her head. "I just wanted to check in with you. I know I went in a little hard on you when you got into the office but I've been worried about you, okay?"

"Christ, everyone's worried about me."

"Everyone?"

"You, Liz."

"How is Liz?"

"Today? She's hungover," Kidd said. "We were out last night. But she's good, yeah. I'll let her know you asked after her."

Zoe smiled. "Thanks." She took a breath. "But seriously, though. You're alright, aren't you?"

Kidd opened his mouth to respond. He was about to be honest with her, about to tell her that maybe he wasn't quite as alright as he was letting on, that maybe he shouldn't even be back at work yet, but he knew that if Zoe knew that, she would find a way to get him back on leave. It wasn't malicious. She wanted what was best for him. So, instead, he fixed a smile on his face.

"I'm happy to be back," he said.

They started out of the car park and past The Pheasantry Cafe. There were a few groups of people sat on chairs outside, Hunter Wellies on, pastel woolly bobble hats with matching scarves wrapped tightly around them. Their focus moved from their overpriced coffee and their overexcited children to the two officers as they walked past. Whispers were exchanged, strong looks, a feeling that they should know what was going on. One of them stepped out in front of them, lightly jogging over from her chair, and fixing a smile so fake and bright on her face, Kidd was practically blinded.

"Sorry, excuse me," she whined. And it really was a whine, the nasality of it cutting through Kidd like a switchblade. "I couldn't help but notice you pulling up just now."

Kidd wanted to say that she probably could have, but where would be the fun in that? People like her lived for moments like this, little moments of drama.

"You're here with the police?"

Kidd cleared his throat, looking down and noticing the lanyard he was wearing, hardly expert detective work on her part. "Perhaps."

"I thought so," she smiled again, the corners of her eyes crinkling, the whiteness of her teeth blinding. "I just wanted to know what was going on?"

"Pardon me?" Kidd asked.

"Well, there are a lot of police cars here," she said, folding her arms. "Is it something we should know about?"

Kidd looked past her to the sea of women craning their necks to hear what they were talking about, to catch a snatch of conversation. Kidd resisted the urge to roll his eyes. He could feel Zoe tensing next to him. She hated this as much as he did.

"Nope, not at all," Kidd said. "Thank you for your time," he added before turning to walk away.

"Um, excuse me," she said again, more forcefully this time. "Ex-CUSE ME."

Kidd stopped and turned back to her. She clearly wasn't used to not getting her way. He forced a smile. She'd be asking for his badge number next.

"Do we need to be worried?" she asked. He couldn't tell if the concern was real or not, or if she was simply trying a different tact to get information. Kidd kept the smile on his face and took a breath.

"Not at all madam," he said. "Please, go back to enjoying your day."

He turned and quickly walked away before she could think of another reason to try and talk to them. It was beautiful in Bushy, it really was. It was a little bit overdone, but that was Richmond for you. It was the great outdoors done to the nth degree, outdoorsy enough for the Richmond mums to feel like they're getting outside when they're not even ten minutes out of town. There was a bloody road that ran through it for crying out loud.

They headed through a gate and into a more heavily wooded area and once out of the winter sunshine, the cold really set into Kidd's bones. There was always something about a crime scene that had a habit of creeping up on him, a chill that crawled up his spine and gripped him like nothing else.

There was a frozen-looking PC at the cordon, his face a little pale, his beard a little wispy. Kidd wondered how long he'd been stood out here. Kidd smiled, nodding at him as they approached, marking himself out as friend rather than foe or nosy passerby.

They showed their warrant cards and walked beneath the police tape, stepping further and further into the trees, further away from civilisation. If Kidd listened really hard, he could hear the road not too far away, the sounds of the world beyond these trees, but only if he really tried to listen. This poor woman would have died alone in the quiet.

They reached the place where the body had been, people dressed in white dusting for prints, taking photographs of the blood spatters, more detailed ones than Kidd had seen that morning.

"The body has already been taken to the pathologist," Zoe said again, zipping up her jacket and tucking her hands into her pockets. The chill of the crime scene was affecting both of them, it seemed. "But you can see the blood spatters," she added. "What do you think?"

Kidd looked back to the entrance to the wooded area. It wasn't particularly well-trodden, most of it overgrown, branches encroaching from the sides. If you didn't know this was here, you likely wouldn't find it.

He turned back to where the body had been. He could picture it in his mind, see the way it had been laid out, the mutilations that had been inflicted. Had there been a struggle? He couldn't tell. In the picture, it hadn't looked like it. So how had it happened?

The route they had taken had been a pretty obvious one, following the paths, but there had to be another way to get to this point in Bushy Park. There were a million pathways in here, they could have taken any one of them. He tried to trace it in his head, getting someone to come through these trees, convincing them to come through here of their own accord? Or carrying a body? Someone would have seen, there had to be witnesses.

"Kidd?" Zoe asked.

"Hmm?"

"Thoughts?"

"There's no way they could have gotten through here without being seen," he said. "Someone has to have seen *something*. Either the victim walking with the murderer or being carried. When we have more information, we need to put out a call for any witnesses."

"Gotcha," Zoe said. "Anything else?"

"They're not a professional," he said flatly. He was repeating himself. The photographs had told him that, but being here now only confirmed it. It was open here, there was too much risk. Hansen didn't do risk, that much he knew. "Who found the body?"

Zoe pulled her phone out of her pocket, clicking a few times before she responded. "Lydia Coles and TJ Bell, two students from Kingston University."

"Can we go and see them?"

"They've given statements."

Kidd smirked. "Not to me they haven't."

CHAPTER
NINE

As they walked away from the crime scene, Kidd already felt a little easier being out of the trees, able to feel the sun on his skin again. He hated wintertime. It always brought out the worst in him. When he was cold, he was irritable, when he was irritable... Well, anyone could tell you he wasn't particularly nice to be around.

Kidd thanked the on-duty PCs as he passed them and they nodded in response. It wasn't much, but chances were they'd been ignored by everybody going in and out of here all day. It was something.

There was a man in a bright orange coat not too far away from where the PCs were stationed. Kidd looked him up and down. He was middle-aged, white, his hair a salt and pepper colour, his skin somewhat withered by the weather. Though his eyes looked youthful, his face had a hundred different stories to tell.

"Find what you were looking for?" he called over.

"Who's that?" Kidd said out the side of his mouth.

DS Sanchez shrugged. "Park ranger. Not met him."

"DI Kidd," Kidd said, reaching out a hand the gentleman gladly took and shook firmly.

"James Doherty," the man replied, putting his hand back into the pocket of his orange jacket. "Terrible business all that, isn't it?"

Kidd eyed him carefully. "Yes," he said. "We're looking into it. I don't suppose you could take us to the Ranger's office perhaps? Would be nice to discuss this further."

"W-w-with me?" James said, his eyes widening, his face suddenly looking all the more youthful, scared almost. Kidd couldn't help but smile.

"Not just you, Mr Doherty. I'd quite like to talk to anyone who would have worked here in the past few days. Shift patterns would be helpful, a sense as to who might have been around," Kidd said. "It's nothing serious." He didn't add the, "Yet" despite it being tempting.

Mr Doherty seemed to calm down at that, taking Kidd and Zoe away from the crime scene and back towards The Pheasantry Cafe. Kidd avoided the gaze of that same group of parents and followed James to a back room where a couple of other orange coats were having lunch. A black woman was wearing a fleece as well as a coat, headphones in, her hands wrapped tightly around a cardboard cup, not paying attention to the two white men sat across the table from each other nursing sandwiches. The men looked up as Kidd and Zoe walked in after Mr Doherty.

"DI Kidd and DS Sanchez are here to look into the… the death in the woods," James said, trailing off a little at the end. "Wants to know who was working at the time."

"And what was the time?" one of the men grunted, having returned to nursing his sandwich.

"We're not sure as yet," DS Sanchez said.

"Course not," the man grumbled.

"But evening seems the most likely," she continued, her teeth gritting a little. "So anyone working nights—?"

"That was likely me then," the man said. Turning around Kidd finally managing to get a good look at his face. He was clearly older than James Doherty, the wrinkles on his face more deep-set, his eyes sunken, bags dragging heavily beneath his eyes. "Anything particular you want to know?"

"Do you mind me asking your name, sir?"

"Petersen," he said. "Evan Petersen."

"And did you see anything happening on the night you were working?" Kidd asked. He wasn't making this easy. "Anything out of the ordinary?"

Evan shrugged. "Nothing out of the ordinary, no," he said. "There were kids around, there always is, university students who don't know they're born. Messing about in the park, the gates don't shut until 10:30 you see, so they were out here, making a nuisance of themselves, leaving a mess that the deer would likely end up picking up. They're terrible."

"But nothing out of the ordinary?" Kidd asked, a little more firmly.

"Nothing," Petersen said. "Same old kids making a nuisance of themselves."

Kidd nodded and eyed Petersen carefully as he returned to his sandwich. He turned to James who gave Kidd an apologetic look.

"Thank you for your time," Kidd said, turning to DS Sanchez. "Shall we?"

They walked out of The Pheasantry Cafe and back towards the car park.

"Right," Kidd said as they made it outside. "That was… odd."

"I'll say," Zoe replied. "He didn't seem keen on telling us anything."

"No," Kidd said. "But that doesn't mean he's guilty."

"No, just a grumpy bastard," Zoe said, looking back towards the cafe. "What now?"

"Off to see our only witnesses," Kidd said.

"I've pretty sure they've told us everything they know, Kidd," Zoe said, somewhat half-heartedly. She knew his mind was made up at this point.

"I'm sure they have," Kidd said. "But it's one thing reading somebody's statement and another hearing it straight from them. I'm not saying whoever wrote it up is bad at their job, I just want to hear it direct. You can't get context from a statement."

"Okay."

"Besides, you said you weren't totally buying what they were selling," Kidd asked as they approached the car park.

"Not a hundred percent," Zoe said. "But, like you

already said, reading a statement is one thing, hearing it from the horse's mouth is—" Zoe stopped as they rounded the corner. There was someone sitting on the hood of Zoe's car. He was a young lad, wearing a pair of jeans and a beanie hat, his dark curls sticking out from underneath it, desperate to be free.

"Christ, what on earth is this?" Kidd grumbled.

The lad must have heard him because he looked up sharply, a pair of hazel eyes wide with panic, hopping off the bonnet with such speed that he was nearly eating gravel. Without missing a beat, he pulled out his phone, and a few quick swipes had him recording Kidd's face as he advanced on the boy.

"Joe Warrington, Warrington's Wonderings," he announced. Kidd's expression didn't shift. He had no idea what he was talking about. Joe noticed. "I'm an online news and entertainment blogger. Heard you were down here to take a look. Didn't you deal with The Grinning Murders case last time around, DI Kidd?"

Kidd blinked and opened his mouth to respond before he registered what the boy had said. How on earth did he already know this was to do with The Grinning Murders case? And how did he know who Kidd was?

"Listen, I don't know what you think you—"

"My name is Joe Warrington," the boy said, slower this time. He was already getting on Kidd's last nerve. "I'm a serious news reporter—"

"You're a prick with a camera who is in my way," Kidd grumbled. "Do you mind?"

"It's just a few simple questions, DI Kidd."

"Then, I impolitely decline." Kidd barged past Joe and towards the car. Joe stumbled in an exaggerated fashion almost dropping his phone. He was recording every second of this, and he was determined to make Kidd look like an asshole. "Zoe? You coming?"

Zoe walked past Joe and climbed into the driver's seat, her face thunderous.

"You shouldn't have done that."

"Done what?"

"Barged him," she said. "Or spoken to him."

Kidd shrugged, pulling on his seatbelt. "Why the hell not? He was in my way. He provoked me."

"He can edit that video to make you look like a bully, Kidd."

Kidd looked at her, incredulous. "Just because I wouldn't talk to him?"

Zoe sighed. "He was filming the whole time. He can do whatever the heck he likes with that footage, edit it, cut it, splice it, you need to be more careful."

Kidd groaned. "It's not my first rodeo, Zoe."

"Really?" she turned in her seat to stare him directly in the face. "Well, maybe you should stop acting like it."

Kidd's mouth dropped open. If it had been anybody else, another DS, a DC, anybody, probably even DCI Weaver, he would have bitten their head off. But this was Zoe. She was only looking out for him.

"Sorry," he grumbled. "I'll do better next time, shall I?"

Zoe rolled her eyes. "Just ignore the prick," she said,

turning the key in the ignition and pulling out of the car park.

———

Zoe pulled up outside the student house and Kidd couldn't help but turn up his nose. His house wasn't exactly Buckingham Palace but this place was borderline slum. With a cursory glance, Kidd could see that the porch door looked like it could be kicked in with pretty minimal effort—more a tap than a kick, most likely—and the front door behind that didn't look like it was in much better shape. The whole house looked like it was falling apart, peeling paintwork on the outside of the garage, what looked like black mould around the single-glazed windows, and plants encroaching on the path leading to the front door. Student houses didn't get much grimmer than this. The landlord was taking these poor kids for a ride, that much was certain.

"Go easy on them, eh?" Zoe said as they walked up the weed-covered pathway to the front door. "They've been through a traumatic experience."

"Living here seems traumatic enough, they should be able to handle a dead body."

"Kidd!"

"I'm joking... sort of," he said, winking at her. "I mean, look at this place, Zoe, it's disgusting."

She shrugged. "Student life."

"Wouldn't wish it on my worst enemy."

Zoe knocked on the door, some flakes of paint falling

with each hit. Kidd stifled a laugh. Zoe dug him in the ribs.

The door was opened by a lanky boy with a clean-shaven face. He was pale, ghostly even, with heavy, dark shadows hanging underneath his eyes, a giant hoodie absolutely swallowing him up. It was practically down to his knees, which was no mean feat considering he could barely fit in the doorframe.

He opened the porch door. It practically fell off its hinges.

"Hello?" he murmured.

"Are you TJ Bell?" Kidd asked.

The boy suddenly looking nervous. Never a good sign. "Yeah, why? Has something happened?"

"You're not in trouble, TJ," Zoe said, though, given his reaction Kidd wasn't so sure about that. She took out her warrant card and showed it to him, Kidd followed suit. "I'm DS Sanchez, this is DI Kidd, he just had a few questions for you and Lydia. Is she home?"

TJ nodded and headed back into the house. Kidd assumed that they were to follow. Manners of kids these days weren't what they used to be.

They stepped into the hallway and Kidd had to stifle a retch. It smelled of damp, the whole place old and falling apart from the inside out. He tried not to look at the corners of the ceiling where black mould was growing at a rate that you could practically see.

"Lydia!" TJ called up the stairs.

"What?" she shouted back.

"The police are here," he called, the slightest quake

running through his voice. A silence seemed to rush through the house like a wave, stopping Lydia from responding like maybe she usually would have. The whole mood in the house seemed to shift, Kidd could practically feel the ground moving beneath his feet.

There were footsteps on the stairs, Lydia coming down in a grey Kingston University hoodie. Her red hair hung loosely around her face, her hands tucked into the sleeves of her hoodie, chipped nail varnish on her fingernails only just visible.

"Is everything okay?" she asked, her voice suddenly soft, so much softer than it had been a few seconds ago. "We gave statements at the police station, I didn't think—"

"Everything's fine," Kidd cut in with a grunt. "Nothing to worry about at all. I just wanted to come and speak to you myself. I was only put on the case this morning and there's only so much you can get from a written statement. I thought it might be nice to chat." Kidd looked about himself. "Do you have a living room we could sit in?"

"No," Lydia said. "There are some chairs in the kitchen." She nodded towards a doorframe at the end of the corridor, no door to be seen. This place just kept getting better and better.

They headed into the kitchen, a pile of washing up in the sink, a mismatched collection of chairs sat around a dining room table. TJ and Lydia sat on one side, Kidd and Zoe took their cue and sat opposite. It all felt a little too much like an interview. Kidd didn't want them to clam up and start getting nervous, but he could see that Lydia was already shaking.

"You're not in trouble, Lydia," he said quietly, his voice coming out a little more like a growl than he would have liked. "Like I said, I just wanted to come here and ask you both a few questions, get your recollection of things just so we can carry on with the investigation. You have nothing to worry about at all."

That seemed to ease her a little bit. At least she would look him in the face now. That was something.

"So," Zoe said. "Do you want to start at the beginning? Tell us about finding the body, how you came to come across it?"

Lydia turned to TJ. He widened his eyes at her. She nodded at him, the two of them speaking in a code that neither Kidd nor Zoe could understand. Kidd had to stop himself from rolling his eyes. If they were going to start off by hiding things, this certainly wasn't going to go well.

"Just the truth," Kidd said, as softly as he could, though Zoe looked at him sharply. He wasn't as good at hiding his agitation as he would have liked. "Like I said, no one is in any trouble."

Yet, he thought.

"TJ found the body," Lydia said quietly. "He saw it and he thought I'd want to see it too. So we both went to see it."

Kidd had to stop himself doing a comedic double-take. He looked at Zoe, who widened her eyes at him sharply.

"Wait," Kidd said. "You found the body, left it there, and went to go and tell your friend?"

TJ shrugged.

"I'm going to need more than a shrug," Kidd said through gritted teeth. "You found the body and..." He trailed off, waiting for the lad to start talking. He seemed reluctant. Something told Kidd that this wasn't in the original statement. "Mr Bell."

"Alright, alright, sorry," TJ said. "I found the body, and it looked interesting, I don't know. I've never seen a body before and this one was... I don't know... it was gruesome. Like something out of a movie, like a horror film or something. So I thought I'd get Lydia because... she's into shit like that."

Lydia scoffed and hit TJ on the arm. "No, it's not like that at all!" Her cheeks were flushing red. "Well, not like he's making it out. I'm not some psycho." She stared daggers at TJ. "I study forensics science at uni," she continued. "TJ thought I'd want to see it because it's something that I'm studying. He thought it might be something I'd want to see in real life instead of just in pictures shown to us by lecturers or whatever."

Kidd watched her closely, looking for a tell, looking for something to tell him that she was making it up, but she just seemed nervous that TJ had put her on the spot. What a dick.

"Okay," he said, turning his gaze away from them, trying not to show his frustration as he waited for the next revelation. "Was there anything else? I take it, this didn't make it into the statement?"

TJ shook his head.

"Well, you'll need to come down to the station and amend that," Kidd growled. "Because at the moment what we have on file is…" he trailed off and turned to Zoe.

"You found the body and called the police," Zoe finished, sighing rather theatrically and sitting back in her chair. Apparently, they were doing Bad Cop, Worse Cop today. "Not the best start."

"Well, that is what happened," TJ said, his voice a little quieter. "It just didn't happen in that order, I guess. There was time in between finding it and calling the police."

Kidd banged his fist on the table. "You're not getting out of this on a fucking technicality," he barked. "This is a murder investigation, son, you need to tell us the truth at all times, otherwise they're going to be looking at you as a suspect."

"What?" TJ looked like he was about to crap himself.

"Well it doesn't look good, does it, Mr Bell?" Kidd said, leaning back in his chair, joining Zoe. *Let's really put the wind up him,* he thought. The chair creaked as he got comfortable, no doubt threatening to fall apart like everything else in this house. "You leave things out of your story, amending your statement, who knows what else you're leaving out, hmm?"

"What? No. There's nothing else," TJ stammered. "It's just that. I know I should have said it but I didn't think it would matter."

"In a murder investigation, *everything* matters," Kidd growled. He knew he was laying it on a little thick now, but at least the lad wasn't likely to lie to him again. Everything would be rosy from now on. "Anything else?"

"It's The Grinning Murders, isn't it?" Lydia said quietly, her voice barely above a whisper.

"What's that now?"

"The Grinning Murders," Lydia said. "I have a professor, Professor Rogers, he talked about it not too long ago, said there was an anniversary or something and it always fascinated him. Then, people have been talking online—"

"Who?"

"Lots of people," Lydia said. "It was trending at one point. News travels fast these days, a picture on Twitter can make it to the other side of the world before you can even blink. All it took was a few people mentioning it and… well… it was him, right?"

"We don't know who it is," Zoe said before Kidd could bite her head off. "This is an open investigation and though there may be similarities, we can't point to anyone just yet. There are a lot of sick people out there, people who would do something like this."

"But it looked a lot like them, right?"

But Hansen is in prison, Kidd thought, staring past the two students at a spot on the faded yellow wall. He'd asked Weaver twice, he'd had it confirmed, and still it was niggling in the back of his mind because he couldn't see it with his own two eyes. Could Hansen be pulling the strings from the inside? Did they even catch the right man in the first place?

He shook his head. Of course, they did. It was iron-clad. Wasn't it? There was that self-doubt creeping in again.

"Anything else, DI Kidd?" Zoe asked.

He pulled his focus back to Lydia and TJ. They both looked a little shell-shocked, like neither one of them had slept in the past few days. He remembered the first time he saw a dead body and it did that to him too. It haunts you.

"Professor Rogers, did you say that was, Lydia?" Kidd asked. She nodded. "Thanks, that will be all." Kidd stood up. "We can see ourselves out. Thank you for your time."

CHAPTER
TEN

"What do you think?" Zoe asked as they walked out of the house. TJ walked them to the door, though he didn't seem to be completely there. He was either stoned out of his mind or terrified that Kidd was going to cuff him and take him in for perverting the course of justice or some such nonsense. Kidd was tempted to do it just so the kid definitely wouldn't lie to them again. But Zoe definitely wouldn't let him get away with that.

Kidd couldn't help but feel there was something a little bit off with him, like he didn't quite know what he was doing. There was a disconnect there that wasn't there with Lydia, that much was for certain. He certainly didn't strike Kidd as a guilty party.

"Annoying that he didn't tell the whole story," Kidd said. "But it doesn't really tell us anything new. Except that TJ's a bit of a twat."

Zoe stifled a laugh. She tucked a strand of hair

behind her ear, the curl immediately bouncing back out and in front of her face. "Looks like we're at a dead-end. At least with those two."

Kidd nodded and they started back towards Zoe's car. "Something like that. I wonder about that professor though."

"What about him?"

"Is it worth talking to him?"

They climbed into the car and Zoe turned to Kidd, the look on her face told him more than words ever could. She didn't think it was a good idea.

"Yeah, I guessed that might be a bit of a long shot," Kidd said, putting on his seatbelt. They were at something of a dead-end here and yet he couldn't shake the feeling that there was something that he'd missed.

There was that creeping feeling in the back of his head that maybe all wasn't quite what it seemed. Or maybe it was just the feeling that his old case, one that he'd dealt with when he was a lot younger, a lot different, had reared its ugly head once more.

"If you want someone to go and talk to him, I'm sure DC Powell could go? It can't hurt."

"Hmmm, maybe," Kidd replied. Zoe switched on the car, the gentle rumble of the engine filling his ears.

He looked up at the ramshackle house and tried to figure out what their next move should be. Even Lydia had been able to see that it looked like Hansen, that the murders bore a striking similarity, even if it was a little more haphazard. Kidd could feel himself spiralling on this one.

Hansen is in prison, he kept telling himself. There was no reason to go and look for him there, he was going to be there, just like he had been there for the last fifteen years. But he still felt like he needed that confirmation, just needed to know that he was still where Kidd had left him all those years ago. It might do something at least to ease his mind.

"I want to go and see Hansen," he said suddenly.

Zoe turned off the car and turned in her seat to look at him.

"What?" Kidd said.

"Albert Hansen?" Zoe said.

"Yes."

Zoe leant back. "You are out of your mind."

"How am I out of my mind?" Kidd protested. "He is the man who killed those three women."

"Fifteen years ago, Ben, he's in prison," Zoe snapped. "He hasn't come out for a day trip and murdered someone in Bushy Park, that's ridiculous."

"I know that," Kidd said, though he didn't completely believe it. He needed to make sure he was still there, for his own peace of mind.

"But you want to go and see him?" Zoe was staring at him, incredulous. If it had been anyone else, he would have just pulled rank, but Zoe was his friend first and his colleague second. "You're just tormenting yourself, Ben, don't do this."

"What harm can it do?"

"*What harm can it do?*" Zoe repeated. "What *good* will it do, Ben? None."

"I want to make sure he's still there," Kidd said flatly. "Don't look at me like that, don't look at me like I'm crazy," he added. She was still looking at him like that. He couldn't blame her. "It might be worth talking to him. For all we know he had accomplices fifteen years ago. Maybe he's got someone visiting him, someone he's telling what to do."

"You're clutching at straws, Kidd," Zoe said.

"I've got to clutch at something," he replied. "You say we're at a dead-end. Well, I need to find us a new route otherwise we're just sitting here waiting for another body to show up."

"We're on the case, Ben," Zoe said. "We're waiting on forensics, we're waiting on DNA to find out who the victim was, we're not just sitting, twiddling our thumbs."

"Well I feel like I need to be doing something," he said quickly. He remembered how it had been last time. Everything had rattled along so quickly in the beginning. They'd barely had a chance to breathe when the first body was found before another one had appeared right on their doorstep. He didn't want another body showing up, he didn't want to have another serial killer on his hands. "He had kids, didn't he?"

"He had a son, but I can't imagine they get on all that well when you consider what Hansen was sent down for," Zoe replied. "I don't think you should go, Ben, Weaver won't like it."

"So?"

"*So?*" Zoe groaned. "Christ, Ben, you've not even

been back for a day and you're about to go and screw it up for the sake of Hansen."

He knew that it wasn't going to be a good move, he knew that Weaver would absolutely blow his top when he found out. But he was more than willing to take that risk for his own sanity. Hansen had haunted him for so long, and now he was managing to do it while he was in prison? Kidd needed to put that demon to rest, and if that meant driving all the way to Belmarsh and pissing off his DCI to do it, then he would.

"I don't care, Zoe, I'm going," Kidd said. "You can either come with me, or you can drop me off at home and I'll take my own car, it's totally up to you. But I'm going no matter what. I have to."

It was clear cut in his mind. He needed to see him there, needed to make sure he was still behind bars. He had to.

Zoe turned away from him, her hands still at ten and two on the steering wheel. She looked like she was about to bang her head on it. Kidd wouldn't have blamed her.

He could practically hear the cogs turning in her head as she stared out at the road ahead of them.

"Fine," she sighed, turning the engine back on. "But I don't like it. I don't like it at all."

"Noted."

CHAPTER
ELEVEN

As they pulled into the car park outside HMP Belmarsh, Kidd could feel his heart rate quicken. He'd not been here for a long time. It looked… almost exactly the same as it did in his mind, just a little older. Maybe it was the grey light from the winter sky, but it was looking a little rundown. To be fair, it had never, in Kidd's mind at least, looked opulent, but right now it looked like it could do with a jet wash. Kidd's heart was pounding hard in his chest as Zoe turned off the engine.

"I'm really not sure about this, Ben," Zoe said. They were the first words she'd spoken to him in the last ninety minutes. Gone was the harsh tone that had been there outside the student house in Kingston. It had been replaced by one of concern. "I don't want you getting into trouble and I don't want you causing yourself any more pain over this."

Kidd sighed. "Look, you're not going to get in trouble for this, it's going to be me," he started. "So don't worry about that. If Weaver finds out, it's my head in the smasher. You only drove me. You were following orders."

She scoffed. "Yeah, I'm sure Weaver will see it that way."

Kidd shrugged. "Besides, I just want to ask him a few questions. It's not going to take more than half an hour." He took a breath and opened the door, the cold wind biting at him as soon as he stepped out of the car. "I won't be long."

"You're going in there alone?"

Kidd nodded. "You're not taking the fall for any of this, Zoe," he said. "I'll be fine. Don't you worry about me."

She raised her eyebrows at him, her way of telling him that she did worry about him, that it was all she seemed to do when they were together. He smiled and slammed the car door.

Kidd walked into the prison entrance and headed to the reception desk. There was a middle-aged mixed-race woman sat behind the desk, her hair curly and a little wild, her bespectacled eyes staring at him intently as he approached. She already seemed completely exasperated by his presence and he wasn't even at her station yet.

This is going to be fun, he thought.

"I'm here to see Albert Hansen," Kidd said, keeping his voice firm, still somewhat struggling to believe those words were coming out of his mouth. He never dreamed he would ever do this. He'd not seen the man in fifteen years, hadn't wanted to see him at any point in the last decade and a half, yet here he was at the man's door.

"I'm afraid visiting hours haven't begun for this afternoon," she said curtly before turning back to her computer screen.

"Can you make an exception?" Kidd asked with a smile. "It's rather important."

"May I ask who you are?" she said, smiling sweetly back at him, but in a way that rubbed Kidd up the wrong way. It felt like she was talking down to him. It probably wasn't the first time someone had shown up asking to talk to a prisoner outside of visitation hours. Maybe she turned a lot of people away.

"DI Benjamin Kidd," he said, pulling out his warrant card and showing it to her. "I just have a few questions for Mr Hansen, if that's alright?"

She raised a careful eyebrow at him in a way that told him she was not at all impressed. It hadn't been his intention to frighten her, he knew what these prison officer types were like, but he thought that mentioning his rank and that he was here to question the prisoner might have held some sway. Instead, she looked as stubborn as ever.

"As I already told you," she said. "Visiting hours haven't begun for this afternoon. You're more than welcome to wait—"

"I won't be waiting," Kidd said, keeping his voice steady. "We can either do this the easy way or the hard way. I can call my boss, he'll call yours, it will be messy. Or you can just let me visit Mr Hansen."

It was a hard card to play, because if she said no, he was screwed. There was no way Weaver would back him on this.

With the pace of a geriatric snail, she started tapping away on her computer. She pulled a book out of the desk drawer in front of her and slid it across the countertop towards him.

"Could you sign in please?" she said, monotonously. "Someone will be along to take you through in a moment."

He signed in, hovering by the desk as he waited for an officer to take him through. He tried to figure exactly what it was he wanted to ask Hansen. This was more than a little bit impromptu and he'd spent the car ride trying not to make too much noise in case Zoe blew up at him again.

Hansen had this way of disarming people when they tried to question him, of being able to turn things around so it was like you were the interviewee rather than the interviewer. He couldn't let that happen this time.

No fewer than five minutes later, a uniformed prison officer was at his side, his eyes tired, his expression a hundred percent bored of this already.

"DI Kidd?" he said.

Kidd nodded and the officer walked away, expecting Kidd to follow, which he did obediently. He was taken through a labyrinth of corridors, of locked doors only accessible by keycards and heavy keys, of bars, to the visiting room where a familiar face was sat alone.

The walls were painted in beige, the kind of colour that was enough to drain the life out of even the bubbliest human. Stationed around the room at regular intervals were tables, a couple of plastic chairs on either side. It was empty, something Kidd hadn't been expecting when they showed up but maybe doing this outside of visitation hours was for the best.

At least this way we can get a little privacy, he thought. Hansen was infamous. If people saw him being spoken to, there would have been questions.

There were prison guards stationed at the various doors in and out of the room, their eyes trained on Kidd, on Hansen. But there he was, as clear as day.

He'd aged considerably since he'd been inside, that much was clear even from a distance. And the years had not been kind. His hair had gotten long, wiry, and grey, hanging lank around his head. He'd let his beard grow, which made him look even older than he was, white with occasional strands of black running through it. But it was his face that had clearly taken the brunt of his time on the inside. His eyes were sunken, making the darkness in them all the more haunting, the wrinkles on his face were pronounced, his lips even seemed to have wrinkled. He'd probably taken up smoking again since he'd been here.

"Well, well, well," Albert growled, his voice was gravelly but it still had that singsong quality just like it had all those years ago. It was a voice that Kidd would never forget. Even now, it sent a chill through his body. "When they told me I had a visitor, I didn't think for a single second it would be you that was coming to visit little old me, DC Benjamin Kidd."

"*DI* Benjamin Kidd," Kidd corrected. "Things have changed since I last saw you."

Hansen looked about himself. "Perhaps they have for you," he replied. "The only thing that's changed here are the inmates. They come and go, I remain."

Good, Kidd thought. That was what he'd wanted after all.

He reached down to pull the chair out only to find it nailed to the floor. Guess they couldn't be too careful. He took a seat across from Hansen, putting his jacket on the blue plastic chair beside him. The seats weren't comfortable, instead they were designed to make you want to spend as little time here as humanly possible, in case the grimness of the room itself didn't already do that to you. Kidd would do his best to keep things brief.

"I wanted to talk to you about the killings," Kidd said flatly, trying to keep his voice as devoid of emotion as possible. He didn't want to give Hansen anything. "The murders."

Hansen looked confused. "Murders from fifteen years ago? Why on earth would you want to do that?"

"Curiosity."

"Killed the cat," Hansen said, a grin snaking across his face. "Maybe it will kill you too."

"You wish."

Hansen laughed. "What is it you want to know?" he asked. "There were so many files, so many transcripts from interview after interview after interview, from the trial, what on earth do you think you could have missed?" Hansen leant forward, regarding Kidd with a careful eye. This was what Kidd had been afraid of. He was already starting to toy with him. "You're not trying to pin something else on me are you?" He grinned, his teeth annoyingly white, annoyingly perfect. The grin that haunted a hundred front pages. "Because I've been in here for the past fifteen years, and believe me, *The Grinning Murders* took up more than enough of my time."

He was almost gleeful at the mention of them. He had a name, he had fame. *Infamy*, Kidd supposed. People had written about him, there had been biographies, there was talk of a TV series about his life, about what he did. It made Kidd sick.

"No, nothing like that," Kidd said, remaining calm, remaining sat back in his chair, not rising to the bait. "I want to know if you've had any visitors. You said you were surprised to see me, were you expecting somebody else? A colleague? An accomplice?"

Hansen laughed. It rang through the empty visitation area and dug itself deep into Kidd's soul. It made him feel cold.

"Oh dear, dear, dear," Hansen said when he composed himself. "You are in a pickle aren't you, *DI* Kidd?" Hansen grinned. Had he stopped grinning since Kidd had arrived? Was this just another piece of attention that he was enjoying? "This is just a checkup, isn't it?"

"Excuse me?"

"Making sure I'm still here, aren't you? Making sure I'm not out there haunting the streets, taking women, slicing their necks open—"

"That's enough," Kidd barked. The prison officers flinched.

Hansen leant back in his chair. "I'm still here, DI Kidd," he said, a hint of glee in his voice. "But I hear things."

Kidd's ears pricked up. "What things?" Was he taunting him? He wouldn't put it past Hansen.

"Oh, all sorts of things," Hansen said, waggling his eyebrows. "I'm assuming that there's someone else out there who fancies themselves the new me, would that be right?"

Kidd stared at him, ashen.

"A copycat, an admirer," Hansen said, picking at his fingernails. "How quaint."

Kidd scrabbled to find the words. He'd read him like a book, just like he always had when they'd been interviewing him all those years ago. He was smart, smarter than people gave him credit for. He always seemed to be able to turn things around, turn the tables. It was maddening.

"Not at all."

"Your silence speaks volumes, DI Kidd," Hansen said with a smile. "I must say I'm flattered that you think I had the time to *train an heir* or however you want to put it. But those murders took up rather a lot of my time, as I already said. I worked alone, as you well know. To suggest anything less is a discredit to me."

Kidd scoffed. Hansen remained stone-faced.

"I cannot help you."

"Cannot, or will not?" Kidd snapped, trying to regain his footing.

Hansen shrugged. "Both."

"You're an arsehole, Albert Hansen," Kidd growled. "Always have been, always will be."

"And you are clueless," Hansen replied. "You think I'm some criminal mastermind from a film, you think you're some kind of vigilante detective. You're not Batman and I'm not your Joker, DI Kidd. What you have on your hands is a copycat and, I assume, nowhere else to turn but me. Am I right?"

Kidd opened his mouth to speak but quickly closed it again. He wasn't wrong. Why had he come here? He wanted to make sure that Hansen was still in the same place he'd left him, still under lock and key, but what else? Did he expect to find he'd been let go? Maybe. That would have made his path ahead clearcut, easy.

"How wonderful that someone wants to emulate me," Hansen said leaning back in his chair, the grin still on his face, the grin that still managed to haunt DI Kidd's worst nightmares even all these years on. "Do you not think so, DI Kidd?"

"No," Kidd replied flatly. "I think it's disgusting. And if I find out you had anything to do with it—"

"You'll what?" Hansen said, the smile slipping from his face, quickly being replaced with a snarl. "You can't lock me up any tighter, Kidd. I'll be in here for the rest of my life. I'll likely die in here. Your threats mean nothing to a man who has already had his freedom stripped away."

"Like the freedom you stripped away from those women," Kidd snapped. "A life for a life."

Hansen chuckled. "Very clever, DI Kidd."

They stared at each other for a moment, Hansen's dark eyes drilling into him just like they always used to. Kidd couldn't take it any longer. He stood up and started away from the table without another word.

As he walked away from Hansen he fought the urge to turn around, to look back at him. But, as ever, his curiosity got the better of him. He turned around and saw Hansen staring at him, unblinking, watching Ben leave him behind.

CHAPTER
TWELVE

D I Kidd was taken back through the long corridors and back to the front desk where the receptionist watched him closely as he signed out.

Hansen was surprised to see me, Kidd thought, wondering, or rather hoping, that there might be something in that. Even if there wasn't, surely it had been worth a try.

He handed the woman back her book, which she gladly took, wiped with an antibacterial wipe, and returned to her desk drawer. She turned back to her computer screen and continued with whatever it was she'd been doing when Kidd had returned. He could see from the reflection in her glasses that she was incredibly engrossed in a game of solitaire. Kidd resisted the urge to roll his eyes at her.

"Can I ask you something?" Kidd asked.

"I think you just did," she replied, clicking her mouse a few more times before training her gaze on him once again. "What can I do for you?"

"I assume you keep all of these sign-in sheets?" he asked.

She seemed a little taken aback, offended almost. "Of course."

Kidd took a breath. "I wasn't trying to insult you," he said. "I only meant that I would like to know who has been visiting Albert Hansen."

She sat up a little straighter. "Hardly anyone at all," she said. "I was a little surprised when you came in asking after him. He doesn't get many visitors. You don't make many friends in that line of work," she added with a little laugh, though quickly stopped when Kidd didn't join in.

"I'd love to know who's coming to see him," Kidd said. "It might be nothing but..." he trailed off. But what?

"It might take a while," she said. "There are an awful lot of names in here. Do you have an email I can send them to?" She handed him a piece of paper which he gladly filled out with DC Ravel's email address.

"Anything you can give me now?" Kidd asked as he handed her back the piece of paper. "If you could flick back through the pages in that little book you've got there and let me know, that would really help me out."

"Well, we get a lot of visitors here, as I'm sure you can imagine," she started, taking the book out of her desk drawer and opening it to the first page. "And Hansen's name doesn't come up in here all that often. The only one I can remember off the top of my head is someone who had the same name as him," she said, shaking her head as she flicked through the pages.

Kidd's blood ran cold.

"Had to be a son or a relative of some kind. Didn't look a thing like him which…" She looked up at Kidd and lowered her voice. "Well, you've seen him, it's a blessing really."

"*Colin* Hansen?" Kidd asked, the name coming back to him in a rush.

That had been the most heartbreaking part of it all, ripping a kid away from a single parent. He always wondered just how much Colin knew about what his dad had done. He was thirteen when it was happening, there was no way he could have been totally clueless, was there? Though, when you're a teenager, if the world doesn't revolve around you, why would you pay attention?

He remembered the day they'd first gone to arrest Albert Hansen and bring him in for questioning. He'd come so willingly it had made it harder to believe he'd done it. Kidd always wondered if he was just impressed that the police had finally figured it out. It had taken them long enough. After that, he'd been let go, and they'd only just managed to stop him before he killed his fourth victim.

Colin had been there when they'd brought Hansen in for questioning the first time, wondering why people were coming to take his dad away. He'd been so confused, a little bit scared, sure, and a couple of officers had stayed behind to look after him. He hadn't needed looking after, he was thirteen years old, but he'd been so distraught.

"That's the one!" the woman said, pointing to the book. "Lucky guess?" she suggested.

Kidd smiled. "Something like that. Would you mind gathering the rest of the visitors and sending it to the office as soon as you have it?"

"No problem," she replied, though it clearly was a problem. It was like getting blood from a stone.

"And CCTV if you've got it?" he added. Every little bit helps.

"I'll get to work on it as soon as I can," she said, putting the book to one side and starting to tap away on her computer. She didn't close the solitaire window, apparently, her game was more important than the lives of the people of his borough.

"Thank you so much," he said, heading for the exit.

He pulled his jacket tightly around himself as he crossed the car park, the wind biting at him with every step. Zoe caught sight of him through the window, her brow furrowing as she saw the look on his face.

He got in the car and she was still staring at him, her eyes burning into the side of his head.

"Well, you did say it wasn't going to take long," she said, looking at the clock on the dash. "But that was fast."

"Hansen was useless," Kidd said, pulling on his seatbelt. "He was still there, but he didn't give us anything new to work with."

"But now that you've seen him, you can put it out of

your head, right? We can carry on with this investigation?"

"Something like that," Kidd said, turning to face her.

"What? What have you found out?" she asked. "You said he was useless."

"He was, but the desk clerk wasn't," he said. "He's had visitors."

"What?"

"Well, one visitor that we know of," he corrected. "She's checking to see who else has been in."

"Who?"

"Colin Hansen."

Zoe's face dropped. "You're kidding."

"I wish I was."

"Jesus Christ."

It looked like Zoe was coming to the same conclusion. Maybe it was too simple, too easy for it just to be his son that was committing these acts, the same acts as his father, but it wasn't so far beyond the realms of possibility that it felt like a long shot. Maybe they should have started there to begin with.

All Kidd knew, as they pulled out of the car park and away from Belmarsh, was that they had a lead, something they could really hang onto. The clock was ticking, and maybe, unlike last time, the cards had fallen in their favour.

CHAPTER
THIRTEEN

I t took them the best part of an hour and a half to make it back to the office, an accident on the M25 and a bunch of rubberneckers slowing their progress considerably. So when they made it back, all eyes were on them.

"Anything?" Owen asked, looking up from his computer. Everybody looked like they were hard at work, DC Powell was finishing off the board, DC Ravel had her head practically buried in her computer, no doubt playing havoc with her shoulders, terrible posture.

"A couple of things, yeah," Kidd said, closing the door behind him. "Weaver around?"

"Had some other stuff to deal with, sir. He thinks the press is starting to get a little antsy," Simon said from the big board, tacking up the last few scraps of evidence from the old case, including Hansen's old mug shot. That was how Kidd remembered him, that little tug of a smile at the corners of his mouth. He couldn't suppress the shiver. "How's the board looking?"

Kidd smiled. "Good, lad, you'll do Owen out of a job."

Owen looked up quickly, opening his mouth to say something but thinking better of it. "What did you get?"

"Spoke to the two students that found the body," Kidd started. "Turns out they actually found the body earlier than they said. The lad, TJ, he found it that morning and then went to get his friend, Lydia, to show her that afternoon, thought she'd find it interesting."

"So the body had been undisturbed for the entire day?" Owen asked.

Kidd shrugged. "I would assume so, yes," he replied. "Which means, in case we needed that confirming, it's a place that people don't often go. If no one found it for an entire day before TJ and Lydia showed up for the second time…" he trailed off.

"He went to get his friend to show her a body?" Owen asked, confusion rippling across his face. "'Hey, I've found a body, do you want to see?' Bit of a weird chat-up line."

Kidd rolled his eyes. "Don't think it was a chat-up line, Owen, think he just wanted to show her the body. Like I said, he thought she'd find it 'interesting.' That's a direct quote."

"Sounds suspect," Owen said.

"Yeah, I thought the same, but she's studying forensics, so I think it might be a genuine curiosity rather than anything malicious," Zoe chimed in.

"But it's weird," Owen said. "Who does that? Should we bring him in?"

Kidd shook his head. "No," he said, bluntly.

"But sir—"

"Drop it."

"Either way," Zoe interjected. "It's worth noting. TJ is going to come in and change his statement, but if we could just make a note of that. Simon?" Simon looked up from the evidence board. "DC Powell, could you please make a note of that?"

"Right away." He scurried over to his computer, practically falling over his own feet, and started typing. "What shall I say?"

Zoe widened her eyes at him before turning to Kidd. "I'm not answering that."

"Just that TJ will be in to amend his statement," Kidd said with a sigh. "And if he doesn't come in, let's say in the next day or so, we'll need to follow up."

Kidd had a feeling TJ wanted to do the right thing. He was pretty sure he'd scared him a little too much about getting arrested for him to leave it as it was. He didn't want to get into trouble. He'd just wanted to show his friend a body. Maybe a little bit weird but no reason to think he was the killer. It would certainly be a bloody weird way to act if he was.

"Did we pick up on anything here?" Kidd asked. "DC Ravel?"

"Waiting for details of the victim before we can do a press conference," she said, looking up from behind her computer. "The boss is keen to beat the press, but we're getting enquiries left and right. Like Powell said, think he's getting it from all sides."

"Not your responsibility," Kidd said. "Don't reply to anyone."

"Yes, sir."

"And can someone look into a Joe... Warrington?" Kidd looked over at DS Sanchez for confirmation. She nodded and rolled her eyes. She may not have been showing it at the time, but he obviously got to her too. "He was hanging around the crime scene. Any information you can get on him might be useful."

"Sure thing," DC Ravel replied.

"What took you so long getting back?" Owen asked. "We thought you'd gotten lost or clocked off and gone to get a pint."

"I'm not you, Owen, we were busy."

"At the crime scene?" Owen asked. "Did you find something new there?"

"Nothing at the crime scene," Kidd said. "Took a trip to Belmarsh."

"Belmarsh?" Ravel chimed in. "Isn't that where Hansen is?"

Kidd looked over at Zoe who simply shrugged.

"Yep," Kidd said, taking off his jacket and hanging it on the coat rack by the door. "Wanted to check he was still there, for my own sanity, and we also got some information out of the clerk that's there. Which reminds me, DC Ravel?"

"Yes, sir."

"I gave them your email address, they should be

sending through a list of visitors in the next couple of days that will hopefully give us an idea of who has been visiting Hansen."

"Why's that, sir?" DC Ravel asked. There was genuine curiosity on her face, she wasn't being facetious.

"We need to start somewhere," Kidd said. "While I was at Belmarsh, Hansen mentioned he was surprised to see me. I took that to mean there have been other visitors. There's one I could do with you tracking down—"

"You were at Belmarsh?" The voice came from the door.

Kidd turned slowly to see Weaver stood in the doorframe, his top button undone showing a little of his chest hair. If he didn't look so furious, and he wasn't twice the size of Kidd in the first place, he probably would have made a joke about casual Friday being moved forward to Thursday or something. But he looked like he wanted to rip Kidd's head off, so he thought he'd keep it simple.

"Yes, sir," Kidd said, trying to keep cool. Well, keep Weaver cool. He couldn't imagine getting reprimanded by the boss in front of his team would be the best look. Plus, it looked like it would be enough to make Powell piss himself.

"To visit Hansen?"

"Yes, sir," Kidd said.

Weaver nodded towards the door, his face like thunder. "Can I have a word?" He didn't wait for Kidd, turning on his heel and exiting the room the way he'd entered.

Kidd looked over at Zoe. Busted.

CHAPTER
FOURTEEN

Zoe shook her head before returning to her desk. Kidd shrugged before following Weaver out of the Incident Room, shutting the door behind him in case Weaver decided to blow his top in the middle of the corridor.

He didn't.

By the time Kidd had closed the door to the Incident Room, Weaver was already halfway down the corridor, storming off towards his office. Kidd sighed, rubbed his fingers against his temples, took a deep breath, and followed. Weaver held the door for Kidd, letting him enter first. He then took his time closing the door, allowing the silence to settle on them both like a fresh coating of snow. It was loud and deadly. Kidd was just waiting for the gunshot.

"Sit down, Kidd."

He took a seat at Weaver's desk, just as he'd done a few hours ago but, in stark contrast to how things had been that morning, now it seemed like Weaver wanted to throttle him rather than welcome him back to the force with open arms.

DCI Weaver paced around the desk and took the seat opposite him, his brow furrowed, a sheen of sweat glistening across his face.

"You okay, sir?" Kidd asked. He wasn't being flippant. Weaver genuinely didn't look okay. That, and the fact he wanted to break the tension.

"You went to Belmarsh to see Hansen," Weaver said, a statement of fact, not a question. Kidd stayed silent. He'd already confirmed it, there was no need for them to labour the point. "Can I ask you what the purpose of that was?"

"The purpose, sir?"

"Yes," Weaver said, sighing heavily. "I'm not trying to trick you here, Kidd. I'm trying to understand what exactly is running through your head right now."

Kidd took a breath, shuffling about in his seat a little. He straightened up, locking eyes with the shark-eyed DCI Weaver and trying to hold his nerve.

"After we went to the crime scene, we took a trip to see the two students who'd found the body," Kidd started. "One of them gave a false statement, by the way, he's going to come in to alter it for us officially, just so you know."

"Right."

"Not false enough to arrest him or anything like that, just a few key details missing because he didn't think they mattered," Kidd said. "But I told him everything matters because this is a murder investigation. Put the wind up him a bit, you know the drill."

"Okay." Weaver's teeth were clamped together. The longer Kidd went on, the higher his dental bill was going to be. Kidd was wondering just how far he could push it before the DCI cracked a tooth.

"I wanted to go and see Hansen," Kidd continued. "He is a very enigmatic man, sir, I'm sure you'll agree with that. I had to make sure, for my own sanity more than anything else, that he was still there under lock and key."

"I told you that he was."

"I know."

"I think I told you that twice actually," Weaver said. "Once over the phone, once in person."

Kid shrugged.

"Like I said, sir, I needed to see it with my own eyes," Kidd replied. "It's nothing personal," he added quickly. "I trust you, I just wanted to see it for myself."

"It's good to hear that you trust me, DI Kidd," Weaver said, his voice heavy, his brow still furrowed, heavy wrinkles stretching across his forehead. "Because you're starting to make me doubt my faith in you."

"Sir?"

"This is a little... against protocol, I would say, Kidd," Weaver said. "I know you have a history with Hansen and a history with this case, but I don't want you going off-piste simply because you feel like it. That isn't how I want things done."

Weaver was staying remarkably calm and Kidd

couldn't place why. Weaver often had a fiery temper. It was something of a running joke in the force because he also had red hair, but this was, in a way, more unnerving. He was doing his best to keep his cool and not give Kidd a complete bollocking and he couldn't understand why.

"Sir, with all due respect, there were prison guards there the whole time, it's not like I went in there and knocked him about or anything. It was just a couple of questions."

"It shouldn't have been *any* questions, Kidd," Weaver said through gritted teeth. He was stoking the fire for sure. It was on the way. The full furnace. "We already have a copycat killer on our hands here, and journalists sniffing at our heels. I don't want anything that could jeopardise this investigation, do I make myself clear?"

Kidd took a breath. He knew it had been a bad idea. He knew Weaver would react like this. That didn't make it any less irritating.

"Crystal," Kidd replied. "Anything else, sir?"

"I'm starting to question whether or not this was a good idea, Kidd," Weaver said, flatly, sitting back in his chair, never taking his eyes off Kidd.

"Oh really?" Kidd said, not allowing his frustrations to show. "Why's that, sir?"

"You're acting erratically, Kidd," Weaver said, laughing a little. "I thought it was a good idea to bring you back early, my neck is on the line here."

"Alright then, sir, if that's the way you feel about it, I'm more than happy to go home."

"Excuse me?"

Kidd shrugged. "I still had about a week left of leave, sir, I'll happily go and leave you to it."

"I don't know what—"

"I was having a lovely time at home," Kidd interrupted, lying through his teeth. "Reading books, catching up on TV shows, do you know how bloody long Game Of Thrones is? Confusing as well. Having to watch most episodes twice to figure out what's going on."

He was overdoing it a little bit and he knew it, but Kidd wasn't having this. Weaver had dragged him back in here because he knew that he was the right man for the job. Otherwise, why would he bother even calling him in the first place? There were other DIs to choose from, DIs that would be able to handle this case no problem. The boss could have done it himself if he'd wanted to, but he'd called Kidd, he needed Kidd, and now he was trying to pull rank.

"Kidd, don't be like—"

"Be like what, sir?" Kidd interrupted. "I'm just telling you that you asked me to come in and do a job, and I'm doing it. We got a lead by going to see Hansen. It might not be much, but it's at least something to go on. It's more than you had when I walked in here—" Kidd checked his watch, dramatic showmanship. "—six hours ago. So, are you going to let me get back to doing my job or do you want another sliced-up body showing up on your patch?"

Kidd knew he was laying it on a little thick but

where was the lie? They'd had one body show up already and they were nowhere close to making an arrest. They could have another one showing up before they knew it, and Kidd didn't want that on his conscience. Not again.

"Y-you did?" Weaver stammered.

"Yes, sir," Kidd said. "I was about to ask DC Ravel to look something up for me before you came in and dragged me out of there wanting a word." Kidd stared his boss down. It would be enough. He knew it would be.

Weaver cleared his throat and sat up in his chair. He shuffled a few papers around on his desk, an indication of busywork, of all the things he needed to do. He mumbled a little and cleared his throat before returning his gaze to Kidd.

"Very well," he said. "Just don't do anything stupid, Kidd. I want you to think before you act."

"I did think, sir," Kidd said, flatly. "I thought that I wanted to go and see Hansen, mostly for my own peace of mind, so I could focus my attention on this case fully and not have him in the back of my head distracting me, so I did it. We got a lead out of it. I'm not about to sniff at that." He sighed. "If it makes you feel any better, DS Sanchez tried to convince me not to do it."

"Did she now?"

"Yes, sir," Kidd said. "So, if nothing else, there's someone in the team trying to stop me going, what were the words you used, sir? 'Off-piste?'"

Weaver cleared his throat, still looking uncomfortable. Kidd had rattled him. Good.

"Well then," Weaver said. "Maybe it's a good thing that you keep working with Sanchez for the time being."

"Of course I'll keep working with her, sir, she's on my team."

"Not what I mean, Kidd," Weaver said, a smile creeping across his face. "She can keep a closer eye on you than I can, so maybe keep that working relationship up and things will be okay."

"Sir—"

"Keep working with Sanchez, keep her in the loop on everything, and maybe, just maybe, listen to her once in a while," Weaver said. "Lord knows you're not going to listen to me, so maybe trying listening to her. You never know, she might end up saving your life one of these days."

Kidd shrugged. He was probably right about that. Sanchez was smart in ways that Kidd wasn't. Where he would rather rush headlong into something, she would think it through and realise that there was a better way to do it, a way that didn't get either of them in trouble.

"Will that be all, sir?" Kidd asked.

"No," Weaver said firmly. "I want this wrapped up as soon as possible, Kidd. I don't want another body. I don't want anyone else getting hurt. We can't have this getting out of hand like last time."

Last time. It made Kidd's blood run cold.

"DC Ravel mentioned a press conference, sir," Kidd said.

"Yes," Weaver grumbled. "The Superintendent wants to have one when we have enough information. Jump on it before the vultures can start printing whatever the hell they like in their rags."

"Understood."

"And I'd like us to have a lead or an arrest by then so they can't nail us to the wall and plaster it all over BBC fucking News."

"Please know that I am doing my best, sir," Kidd replied. "It might seem unorthodox but there is a method to the madness."

Weaver raised an eyebrow at Kidd. "I should bloody hope so, because right now I'm seeing more madness than method, DI Kidd. Don't let it continue."

CHAPTER
FIFTEEN

Having been dismissed, Kidd managed to bite his tongue until he made it outside of Weaver's office and closed the door. He was surprised to see Zoe stood waiting for him, leaning against the wall opposite. She'd untied her long curls so they were now hanging down on either side of her face. She looked more relaxed than she had earlier, less severe somehow, the mane softening her. That's probably why she tied it up for work most of the time. She didn't want to look soft around all the macho police bullshit that happened in this place.

She had two disposable coffee cups in her hands. Without a word, she handed one to him.

"Thanks," he said, taking a quick sip. Coffee. Splash of milk. Two sugars. She still remembered. Not that it was hard to forget, but it was the thought. "Perfect."

He let out a breath and leant on the wall opposite Zoe.

"You look beat," she said in a low voice.

Kidd held back a yawn, his eyes watering. "Being back on the job is more knackering than I remember," he grumbled, taking another sip of coffee. "And Weaver being Weaver is also a thing I forgot about. Thanks for this, definitely needed."

Zoe shrugged. "Don't mention it."

They started down the corridor away from Weaver's office.

"How'd it go?" she asked as they walked. "I didn't hear him yelling, so I assume he didn't exactly give you the hairdryer treatment."

"How long were you out there?" Kidd asked.

"Waited five seconds and followed you down the corridor," she said with a shrug. "If he was going to go full Fiery Freddie Weaver on you I wanted to hear it."

"So you're leaving disappointed?"

"Devastated!" she said, clutching a hand to her chest dramatically. "So, no bollocking?"

Kidd snorted. "No. I get the feeling he wanted to though. He wasn't impressed with the Hansen situation."

Zoe gasped. "No, really? You don't say. I didn't see that coming at all."

Kidd fixed her with the harshest glare he could muster, but it only made Zoe crack up. If it had been anyone else, he probably would have emptied his coffee over them. In fact, if this coffee hadn't been the very nectar of the gods, he even would have done it to Zoe Sanchez at that moment.

He sighed and took another sip. "He wants you to keep an eye on me."

Zoe's face wrinkled in disgust. "Ew, really?" she replied. "That's... I don't know." She thought about it for a moment. "That seems pretty patronising to me, Ben."

"Glad you think so," Kidd replied. "And glad to know we agree, because he wants you to grass me up if I'm acting like a knob."

"Grass you up? What the hell does he think this is?" she replied. "I wouldn't, just so you know," she added. "You're not doing what you're doing because you're some macho dickheaded DI, you're doing these things because you give a shit and because you want this case solved."

DI Kidd looked over at her. She shrugged. "What?"

"Just glad you don't see me as some macho dick-headed DI."

"I don't even see you as macho," she replied, taking another sip of her coffee. "Christ, this is good coffee."

"You'll have to tell me where you get it from," Kidd replied. "The days are going to be long and frankly, I'm not drinking the shit they have here. It's this or I'm out."

"Hey, none of that talk, I'm your keeper now," Zoe said, waggling her eyebrows. "You'll drink whatever coffee flavoured swill you're given and you'll like it."

"You're enjoying this far too much."

"What?" Zoe gasped. "Me? That doesn't sound right, not at all."

"Could you enjoy it just a little bit less?" Kidd said, a grin tugging at the corners of his mouth.

"I will, if you will," she replied, leading him back into the office. Unlike last time, DC Campbell, DC Powell, and DC Ravel all averted their gaze as he walked in. Maybe they thought he'd be in an extra foul mood after being reprimanded and be on the warpath. Either way, he appreciated them not prying for gossip.

"What's next, boss?" Zoe asked.

"Don't call me boss," Kidd replied. "You know I hate that."

"Will you call me boss?"

"Will you tell me where the good coffee is?"

"I'll consider it," she said, returning to her desk. She took her seat and turned on her computer. Kidd remained standing, watching her closely. She took a deep breath. "So, seriously, what's next?"

"We've got a lead," Kidd said. "We can go and talk to Colin, see what he's been going to see his dad about, and then… well, we see what he has to say and we move on from there."

"Okay, that's a start."

"Ravel," he called across the room, turning to where she sat at her desk. She looked up sharply.

"Yes, sir?"

"Any word from the pathologist on who the victim is?" he asked.

Ravel nodded, turning back to her computer and making a few quick clicks. "I would have brought it up when you came in, sir, but you were busy and then you got dragged out by Weaver and-"

"It's okay," Kidd said, crossing the room to her desk. "What have you got for me?"

Ravel turned the screen to Kidd and he read what was written. For the second time that day, Kidd felt his blood run cold.

"What?" Zoe asked from across the room. At the look on Kidd's face, she got up and crossed the room to look at the screen alongside him. "Jennifer Berry," she said flatly. "Why do I know that name?"

Kidd was thrown back a whole fifteen years, to when he'd gone to a house with the liaison officer and seeing the look on a young girl's face as they told her that her mummy was never coming home. Angela Berry's husband was completely crushed but trying to stay strong for their little girl, who was absolutely torn apart by the news.

Kidd sighed. "Jenny Berry was the daughter of one of Hansen's original victims."

CHAPTER
SIXTEEN

Zoe blinked. "Wait a minute, a relation?"

Kidd growled and walked over to the evidence board. He looked to the first drop, where all of the details of the first murder were but was met with the wrong face. That was Natalie Anders.

He moved along to see the second victim. Angela Berry. She was in her early forties, had worked at the same company as Hansen, they'd been great friends apparently but she had a troubled life with her husband. When she'd gone missing, everybody assumed it was the husband or that she'd left him, then her body showed up dumped by the river just a few weeks later.

Kidd's mind started to spiral as he looked from Natalie Anders over to Angela Berry. How much of a copycat was this murderer?

"What are you thinking?" Zoe had appeared at his side, looking up at the same pictures he was.

"I'm trying to figure it out," he said. His head was

spinning with so many questions that he was trying to get a handle on just one, trying to order his thoughts so he knew exactly what to do next. "How closely do you think our copycat is following the script?" Kidd asked.

It wasn't a question that necessarily needed answering right this second, but Zoe thought about it for a moment before responding.

"If they're copycatting the style of murder," she said cautiously, "then there is nothing to say that they wouldn't also try to copycat the victims too." It was what Kidd had been afraid she'd say. "Does that mean what I think it means?"

Kidd nodded. "It means that if our killer is following the same pattern of people as Hansen did, then 1) a member of Natalie Anders' family could be in serious trouble and 2) someone needs to get in touch with Karen Nicks' next of kin." He turned back to the team. "You hear that?" he called. A series of nods came back to him. "It's very possible that there is another body *somewhere* on the borough, so I need somebody to try and get in touch with Natalie Anders' family."

"On it, sir," DC Ravel volunteered, darting back to her computer and furiously attacking the keys on her keyboard. It was a sound that normally annoyed Kidd, that constant clacking, but right now it was music to his ears. It was progress, every tap on that keyboard was getting them closer and closer to catching this murderer.

"If you could also check in with Karen Nicks' next of kin, that would be fantastic," Kidd said, sending a thumbs-up her way. She sent one back without looking up.

"Anything for me to do, sir?" Powell piped up, ever the eager beaver.

"I'm going to need somebody to go with a liaison officer to tell Jennifer Berry's family that she's been murdered," Kidd said solemnly. He didn't want to send someone so young into the fire like that, but maybe if Owen went with him it wouldn't be so bad. "Go with DC Campbell, find out anything you can about the daughter, anything that might give us a lead."

"Righto, sir," Owen said.

"Be sensitive," Kidd barked.

Owen stepped back. "I'm always sensitive."

"Like fuck you are," Kidd replied. "Keep him in check, Powell, won't you?" He winked at DC Powell who looked like he was about to collapse.

Kidd looked back at DS Sanchez who was eagerly awaiting her orders, possibly even more so than Powell. She was ready to get going on this as much as Kidd was. As sick as it might have sounded, the information had lit a fire under both of them and they were ready to get this done.

"You're with me, Sanchez," Kidd said with a shrug. "Weaver's orders."

"We going to check in on Colin?"

"Yep," Kidd said, about to head to the door when he turned back to the team. "One thing I was going to say before Weaver rudely interrupted me earlier on, we have a suspect." The room went quiet as they waited for him.

"Don't get too excited, it could be a dead-end, but Hansen has been getting visits from his son. That was the only person that the clerk at Belmarsh could remember, so he'd been there enough for it to stick in her mind. It's a long shot, maybe too obvious, but DS Sanchez and I are going to go and have a word with him, see what information we can get out of him. If anything."

Kidd turned back to the door, grabbing his jacket, and slinging it over his shoulders. He was about to open the door when DC Ravel squeaked from behind her computer. He spun around so fast he nearly knocked over the coat stand.

"What?" he called across the room.

DC Ravel stood up. "Pathologist report," she called back. "Body was cold around sixty hours. So time of death is considered to be some time on Monday night."

Kidd rushed back to the board and started to do some quick calculations in his head, marking back the dates, seeing just how long they had before the killer might be likely to strike again.

He turned to the team, his voice dark. "I'd wager we have about two days before another body shows up," Kidd said, eyeing each of his team in turn. "The faster we figure this out, the more likely we are to save a life," he added, before turning back to Zoe. "Let's go. We don't have time to waste."

They hurried down the corridor towards Weaver's office. Kidd wasn't sure if he'd want to know what was going on, but decided to keep him informed, even if it was just to score points against the miserable bugger.

He didn't knock, pushing the door open with such force that Weaver practically jumped out of his skin.

"You scared me half to death, you prick, what do you want now?" he barked.

Aha, there's that fire, Kidd thought.

"Off to see Colin Hansen, sir," Kidd said. "Thought you might want to know. Plus we've got a DNA match on the body. Jennifer Berry."

Weaver's face screwed up. "Why do I know that name?" And then it dawned on him all at once, just as it had done for Kidd a few moments ago. His mouth fell open. "You're joking."

Kidd shook his head. "Be a shit joke if I was, boss. DC Powell and Campbell are going to speak to the family now, and DC Ravel is looking up the family members of the other victims to see if... well... to see if anybody has gone missing recently."

"You really think—?"

"I don't know what I think, sir," Kidd said. "But I'm not ruling out the possibility that this nutcase isn't just following Hansen's methods but he's following his victims too. We're going to see Colin Hansen."

"Don't be a hero, Kidd."

"Never do, sir." He slammed the door and marched down the corridor with Zoe at his side.

CHAPTER
SEVENTEEN

Zoe Sanchez pulled out of the car park at breakneck speed, barely giving Kidd a chance to get his seatbelt on. He resisted the urge to swear as she swung out onto the road, nearly straight into a cyclist with no pissing lights on and no high-vis.

"We need to get there in one piece, Zoe, maybe don't drive like a twat."

"Maybe learn to drive before you start telling me how to do it," she grumbled, pulling out of the high street and heading out of Kingston and over Kingston Bridge towards Richmond borough.

"You know where you're going?"

"Of course, I bloody do." She snorted. "I had DC Ravel check out Colin's address while you were getting a bollocking from Weaver. Grabbed it on the way out the door."

He looked over at Zoe whose eyes were fixed squarely on the road. This was what they had been like before Kidd had been sent on leave. Zoe Sanchez was a bloody good DS. It was a wonder she hadn't been made a DI yet, though that was something Kidd was glad of. He enjoyed working with her and the day she became a DI, she'd be off being SIO on her own cases without him. It would happen one day, but he was glad it hadn't happened yet.

They got lucky with the traffic. If they'd have left any later, they would have been caught in the rush hour and Kidd would be itching to be anywhere but in the car.

Zoe sped through Hampton Wick, beneath the railway bridge, and towards Teddington Lock, Kidd suddenly having an idea as to where they were going.

"Lower Teddington Road?" Kidd asked, somewhat hesitantly.

"Yeah," Zoe replied as she turned off again, slowing down as the speed limit shifted in the residential area. She was craning her neck to look out of the windscreen, the veins in her neck popping as she drove. "How'd you guess?"

"Not a guess, Zoe," Kidd replied. "What number is it?"

She told him and Kidd found himself staring out the window, watching the houses go by, the houses that he knew pretty well. It wasn't every day that his job brought him down this road, but whenever it did it was enough to send a chill through his bones.

"Why are you being weird?" Zoe asked. "What's wrong with the address?"

"That's Albert Hansen's house."

"Colin Hansen."

"No, Zoe, you're not hearing me," Kidd said. "Colin is living in his old family home. I don't know why it didn't occur to me that he would. His dad would have probably left it to him when he went to prison. Why wouldn't he stay in a fancy house on the river in Teddington?"

Zoe eyed him carefully from the driver's seat. "So, this is the house that you came to fifteen years ago when you took Hansen away?"

"Uh-huh," Kidd replied. And it was the same house he'd had to come to with somebody to tell Colin everything that had happened to his father, that he was going to be in prison for a while—he'd underplayed it, of course, the lad was only thirteen—and did he have a member of his family to come and stay with him or that he could go and stay with? They'd never checked up on him after that, at least Kidd hadn't. It hadn't felt like it was his place to.

"You feeling okay, boss?" Zoe asked, reaching for the joke they'd had just a little while before, but missing it by a mile. Kidd was elsewhere.

"Don't call me boss," he mumbled. "And I'll be fine, yeah. Everything about this is setting me on edge. Every other hour I seem to be sent on a trip down memory lane." And the memories weren't ones Kidd was keen on revisiting. He was so much younger at the time, barely out of uniform, and he was working on a case like that.

Zoe pulled up outside the house and it took all of Kidd's strength not to make a noise when he saw the house. It looked almost exactly the same as it had fifteen years ago. The white door to the garage looked like it had been freshly painted, the patio looked jet washed and perfect, picturesque ivy climbed up the red bricks outside the house. It was the perfect little suburban home, and there had been a vicious murderer in there the whole time. He wondered if they were about to prove the same thing again.

The only thing that was different were the hordes of people on the pavement. Kidd hadn't noticed them at first, but they'd noticed him, a couple of them pointing, one or two raising their cameras to get a good look at him and snap a shot just in case he happened to be someone important.

The flash made Kidd wince.

"Christ, what's all this then?" he grumbled.

Zoe sighed. "Looks like we're not the only people with an interest in Colin Hansen," she said, looking past Kidd at the crowd. She turned off the engine and undid her seatbelt. "Last chance to bail and send somebody else in there, Ben."

Kidd shook his head. "No chance," he said. "Are you ready for your close-up?"

"If I end up on a front page and I look shit, I'll sue."

"There's a joke in there somewhere," Kidd said.

"And if you make it, I'll run you over," Zoe quipped.

They got out of the car and a couple of people from the crowd moved towards them. He looked and saw press badges, though no faces that he recognised, nothing more than the local papers and freelancers trying to get a bit of information, anything to sell a rag.

Kidd walked towards the front door, keeping his eye-line above them and focused on the house as much as possible. There were a couple of people shouting questions that he couldn't quite make out, a layering of voices that made him want to rip off his own ears.

"What can you tell us about why you're here?"

"Is Colin Hansen a suspect?"

"Any further leads on *The Grinning Murders* case, DI Kidd?" That last one caught Kidd's attention. The use of his name, a voice he'd heard for the first time earlier in the day.

He turned sharply to his left to see Joe Warrington stood in front of him with his phone held out like a microphone. He'd let his curls free so they looked a lot wilder than they had done under his hat, but was still wearing the same hoodie and jeans he'd had on earlier. Had he just gone from Bushy Park to here? It wasn't exactly far. All just to stand outside and harass Colin Hansen?

"Move," Kidd growled, but Warrington seemingly heard, "Please come and stand directly in my path," because he did just that, positioning himself right in front of Kidd as if he was giving an impromptu press conference.

Absolutely not, Kidd thought.

"Running out of options so pointing the finger at the son?" Warrington's eyes were glinting with something akin to pride at that one. He was smiling, flashing his slightly crooked teeth at Kidd. "Is that silence a confirmation?"

"That silence is—"

"Just silence!" Zoe interrupted, grabbing hold of Kidd's arm and marching him towards the front door. The crowd followed them, clamouring louder now, asking more questions, Warrington practically tripping over his own feet just to stay at the front of the pack.

The porch light flicked on, bathing the two of them in an orangey glow in the fading light of day.

"At least he fixed the porch light," Kidd said.

"What?"

He pointed up to the orange light above their heads. "The whole time we were investigating before, the porch light was out. Colin must have fixed it."

Ignoring him, Zoe knocked on the door as hard as she could, the gold door knocker jumping with every impact, the glass panes shuddering. There was no answer. There were lights on in the house, a car on the driveway, he was obviously here. People had probably been knocking his door down all day, trying to get a picture of him, trying to get him to answer some far too cleverly worded question designed to trip him up. These journalists, if you could even call them that, were scum.

"No answer," Kidd said.

"Can't imagine why," Zoe snarked.

Kidd bent down and opened the letterbox with his fingers. There was a bark in return that made him jump back.

"Skittish!" Zoe commented.

"Don't fancy losing a finger," Kidd replied. "You're more than welcome to try if you like?"

Zoe held her hands up, so Kidd bent down again, opening the letterbox and trying to keep his fingers as far from harm as possible.

"Colin? It's DI Kidd from Kingston Police," he called, doing his best to be heard over the dog's yapping. It was definitely more of a yap than a bark, perhaps not the most threatening of beasts, but enough to startle anyone who wanted to try and break-in. "Could you let us in? We won't let any of the vultures inside."

There were footsteps inside, the sound of a door opening and closing, and through the gap in the letterbox, Kidd could see a pair of legs coming their way.

"Out of the way, Buzz," Colin hissed. "Get in, go on, go and lay down."

Kidd let the letterbox fall closed and stood back up, drawing up to his full height. The door opened and in front of Kidd stood Colin Hansen. The blasts from the past just kept on coming.

He looked exactly as he had all those years ago, just supersized. Instead of being a little bit gangly and spotty, he'd filled out a little, probably from regular visits to the gym. Rather than the same dark curls as his father, he had his dark hair cropped close to his head and his eyes didn't have that same shark-eyed quality. He had, according to Albert, his mother's eyes, which were a much gentler light brown colour.

He looked like he had hardly slept, the purple bags weighing heavily under his eyes. His lips were a little cracked and as he looked out at Kidd a moment of recognition passed across his face.

"It's you," he said in a whisper. He always was quite well-spoken, Kidd could remember that much. He'd been so polite to the officers that had come to his door on that night fifteen years ago, offered them tea, all sorts. As Kidd regarded him, it seemed hard to believe that this man could be responsible for the same atrocities as his father. It didn't sit right with him.

"That's right," Kidd said. "I thought you might remember. I'm DI Kidd, this is DS Zoe Sanchez," he added. "Do you mind if we come in?"

The flashbulbs on the tops of the cameras started going at an alarming rate. Colin's eyes widened as he sank back into the house.

"I'd prefer it," he said, shielding himself behind the door. "Please come in. Don't mind Buzz, he's a loud-mouth but he's harmless."

"Sounds like Weaver," Zoe muttered.

Kidd and Zoe stepped through the doorway and Colin quickly closed the door behind them. Through the glass panes on the front door, Kidd could see the flash-bulbs still going, like Colin was about to come out for an encore. They calmed down a few moments later and the crowd went back to waiting.

"They been hanging around out there all day?" Zoe asked.

Colin nodded, looking utterly exhausted by it all. "They think they have the inside scoop on everything that is going on," he said. "All it took was one person mentioning that the killings were like... well, like my dad's and suddenly they were all here trying to get an exclusive."

"Can't be easy," Zoe said.

"No, it's not," he said flatly. "And I assume that's why the two of you are here also, is it not? Think you've got the measure of my dad and therefore got the measure of me."

Kidd sighed. "I wouldn't put it like that exactly," he said. "We just have a few questions for you, Mr Hansen, if that's alright?"

As he looked at Colin Hansen, a man who was nothing like his father, Kidd started to have his doubts. Back at Belmarsh, he'd felt that sudden twist in his gut at the mention of Colin's name, the possibility that they'd found themselves a viable suspect, but now that he was here, he wasn't so sure.

Kidd tried to shake it from his head. That's what things had been like all those years ago with Albert— they'd all been fooled by him and that had ended with another body. He wasn't about to have another life on his conscience.

"Not a problem," Colin said, pointing his hand in the direction of a door to his right. "The living room is just through there. Would either of you like a drink?"

"I could murder a cuppa," Zoe said quickly.

"Same here please, Colin," Kidd said.

Colin headed off through a different door and Kidd followed Zoe into the living room. Kidd took it all in, his eyes wide as he remembered being here fifteen years ago. He'd not stepped foot inside since. He'd not even bothered to check up on him.

"What now, Kidd?" Zoe whispered. "Are you amazed at the redecoration?"

"Piss off," Kidd grumbled. "What do you think?"

"Of the decor?" Zoe replied before shrugging. "It's okay I guess. Not the colour I would have chosen for the walls—"

"Not the bloody walls, Zoe." Kidd groaned. "Of Colin."

"Colin seems pretty docile," Zoe said. "I don't know what I expected, to be honest. Maybe someone who didn't want the police in his house, but wasn't Albert accommodating in the beginning?"

"That's the only thing giving me pause," Kidd replied.

The dog, a tiny, yappy Basset Hound, was running around Zoe's feet whimpering, which was enough to make Kidd want to kick it. He didn't condone violence against animals, but this one was so irritating he was almost willing to make an exception.

Zoe crouched down and started fussing with him, rubbing behind his ears and across his back, the yapping suddenly turning into excitable pants and sighs, a big pink tongue flopping out of his mouth.

"Well aren't you just the cutest little thing?" Zoe cooed.

"Didn't know you were a dog person, Zoe."

"Not usually," she said. "But for this cutie pie? Maybe I am."

"Jesus Christ."

"I won't have dog hate on my watch, boss," Zoe said. "I won't stand for it."

"How about you stand outside then?"

"Heartless old grump."

Colin walked into the living room with two mugs in one hand and a third in the other, all of them steaming. Kidd could already taste the sweet nectar of tea before he was even anywhere near it. He was practically salivating.

"Thanks, Mr Hansen," Kidd said, taking the two mugs Colin proffered.

"Please, call me Colin, DI Kidd," Colin replied. "We've had far too much history for you to start being so formal with me." He pointed to the sofa. "Please, sit."

Kidd handed Zoe her mug and the two obliged, sitting side by side on the cream leather sofa. Colin put his mug down on a coaster before going over to the bay window and making the sure the curtains were pulled tight. Probably not the first time he'd done that today. Kidd felt sorry for the poor bastard.

"So, Colin," Kidd began, "I hope you don't mind us popping round—"

"When I heard, I expected it would happen sooner or later," he said, crossing the room back towards his tea and taking a seat in an armchair. He cocooned the mug in his hands, occasionally blowing over the top of it despite not taking a sip. It must have been a nervous habit. When the last time police were in your house was to tell you your dad had been arrested, that had to be something of a triggering experience.

"When did the people outside arrive?" Kidd asked.

"A day or so ago," Colin said. "I returned from work on Tuesday to see that my house was swarming with them. I thought something had happened, there'd been a break-in or something, but they were firing questions at me about dad and I had no idea why." He took a sip of his tea, wincing at how hot it still was. "Then I got inside, did a little bit of googling, and figured it out. They've been there every day since."

"Constantly?" Zoe asked.

Colin chuckled. "No, not constantly. They sort of come and go. But I... I haven't wanted to leave the house since they got here. They're quite aggressive," he said, eyeing Kidd. "I think you saw that on the way in."

"Yes," Kidd replied. "Persistent, too."

Colin rolled his eyes. "Certainly. I've worked from home since then. Only two days, but it's driving Buzz mental only having the garden to run around in and, frankly, it's driving me a little bit nuts too. I could do with a walk, with seeing something other than the inside of this house."

It was a pretty big house. Kidd remembered how long it had taken them to search it all those years ago. How could you go mental when you had all of these rooms to play about in? If it had been his house back in Kingston, maybe, but here? Kidd honestly couldn't see it.

"Seeing as you know why we're here, Colin, there's

no point in us beating around the bush," Kidd said, clearing his throat. "We are here to talk about your dad." Colin winced. He'd not even mentioned his dad's name and it was enough to cause a visceral reaction in him. Could he have done it? Or was he just that good of an actor? "Have you been to visit him much?"

Colin's eyes widened. "Excuse me?"

"Simple question, Colin. I just wanted to know if—"

"I know. I know, I heard what you said, I just can't believe you said it," he grumbled, taking his eyes away from Kidd and staring at the cream carpet. "You really think I'm going to see that man?" Colin said quietly. "After everything he did? He drove my mum away when I was a child, and then to do all of those things to those women…" Colin trailed off. He took a breath and composed himself, returning his steely gaze to Kidd. "I've not been to see him, not once in the past fifteen years," Colin said flatly. "Anything else?"

"Colin, I didn't mean to offend you," Kidd said. "We just had reason to believe that you'd been to Belmarsh to see your dad over the past few weeks—"

"Which automatically made you think that I was going along there to get tips on what to do with the next body, huh?" Colin spat. "Seriously?"

"We have to take every lead we get seriously, Mr Hansen," Zoe said softly. "You understand we're only doing our jobs here."

Colin took another breath, quickly followed by another sip of tea. "Of course, I understand," he said. "Please, carry on."

"If not you, could it have been another member of your family going to visit?" Kidd suggested. Maybe the receptionist had gotten the first name wrong. Maybe it was a different Hansen. "Is that beyond the realm of possibility?"

Colin smiled at Kidd. "I'm afraid so," he said. "Neither of my aunties would go, I'm fairly sure of it. And my nan is long since passed. Not many Hansens remaining now."

Kidd sat back in the sofa, suddenly floored at how they'd found themselves back at square one all over again. He knew it had all felt a little bit too easy for it to be Hansen junior. But if not Colin, then who?

"I'm sorry to disappoint you, DI Kidd," Colin said. "You know I'd love to help you if I could. Though, if you fancy doing me another favour, you could always have that filmmaker kid arrested. Don't suppose you've got any drugs to plant on him or anything?"

Kidd sat up sharply.

"Mr Hansen—" Zoe started.

"I'm joking, please don't put that on any record. I don't want him getting in trouble, not really," Colin chuckled. Buzz trotted over and hopped up onto Colin's lap. He stroked the dog absentmindedly, ignoring the dog as he gnawed at his jeans.

"No, no," Kidd said. "What was that about a filmmaker?"

Colin looked him dead in the eyes. "He giving you trouble too?" Colin asked. "Little shit-stirrer thinks he's the next Trevor McDonald. He's not even close."

"Why? What's he done?"

Colin shook his head. "Just been himself, I think," he said with a laugh. "Saw him last week because he was asking me questions about my dad, about all the things he'd done, wanted to make a documentary about it or something. He's studying film at uni, I think. I started off being helpful, how could I not? He's just a kid. The next thing I know, he's out there rallying the troops. Posted everything I said online, making me out to be some kind of villain. He's probably loving it. Imagine all of this shit in his film. He starts making it and a body shows up?"

Kidd took a deep breath, not wanting to spook Colin or the dog.

"Can I get the lad's name, Colin?"

"Joe Warrington."

CHAPTER
EIGHTEEN

J*oe bloody Warrington*, Kidd thought. He knew he was trouble. How could he not be, with the way he was carrying on at Bushy Park? The way he'd been with Kidd out in front of Colin's house? But was he a killer?

"Deep breaths, Ben." Zoe's voice came from next to him, calm as anything, but she was sat forward on the sofa just like he was, her right leg jiggling an unsteady beat. "Don't jump to any conclusions."

"How long has this been going on?" Kidd asked, trying to keep his voice level.

Colin looked a little bit surprised at how the mention of Joe's name had been taken. Suddenly a little bit sheepish, Kidd could see him clamming up before his very eyes.

"I don't want any trouble. I was just making a joke. I'm not about getting people into trouble if—"

"No one is in trouble yet, Colin," Kidd said. "But if

Warrington has been asking you questions and suddenly a body shows up, it just seems… suspicious."

"He's just a student."

Kidd shrugged. "You'd be amazed at what people are capable of."

Colin took another sip of tea. Kidd was fairly sure the mug was empty at this point and it was a nervous habit, but he couldn't prove that, short of knocking the mug out of Colin's hand.

"Colin?" Kidd's voice had a hint of a warning in it. Zoe stiffened next to him.

"He was asking me about my dad," Colin said simply. "All sorts, really. He asked what happened, how many bodies there were, how he did it. I didn't know the last bit, of course, but I gave as detailed an answer as I could, because, well, he's a university student. He's just doing what he can to get a degree and he obviously wanted an interesting short film about me… about my family…"

Colin trailed off and Kidd eyed him carefully. He had no reason not to believe him. Why would he? Colin had been honest with them since they got here, why would he stop being honest now? But Kidd could see that hint of his father in those final words.

Albert Hansen had always been after the infamy, the accolades. Maybe there was a part of Colin that wanted that too. He'd been approached in the past for TV shows about his dad, them no doubt wanting the sordid details on how it managed to tear a young boy's life apart. He'd even done a few of them. But why now? Why again? Why had he done it for Warrington?

"And you answered all of his questions?"

"As best I could, yes."

"And he filmed them all?" Kidd asked.

"Yes. He had a little camera set up in the corner and sat where you're sitting now, and I sat in this chair with Buzz, sometimes without, he can be fussy like that, and I just talked."

"You just… talked?" Kidd was getting irritated now. How much did Warrington know? How much had he asked? Was this information he'd used to kill someone? Could Hansen have provided that? "About what, Colin? What did you say?"

"I told him all sorts," Colin said, flustered now. "Things I'd read in the papers mostly, articles. Dad never told me that he was doing any of that stuff, never gave the gory details, so I was just regurgitating stuff I'd read over the years."

"Why?"

Colin opened his mouth to speak and stopped himself. He lowered his voice considerably. "Because it would make for a more interesting documentary," Colin said. "I told him it was all from articles, things that I'd read over the years, TV shows I'd watched and been part of, it was all… it was all information that was out there…"

Colin trailed off and looked between Kidd and Zoe, a panicked expression on his face. He looked like he was about to pass out.

"Thank you, Colin," Kidd said gruffly. "You've been very helpful."

He stood up. Zoe joined him.

Colin moved to stand up but Kidd stopped him with a wave of his hand. "We can see ourselves out," he said. "No use you getting those vultures all riled up. Thank you for your time, Colin."

"Y-y-you're welcome…" he said quietly, turning his attention back to his dog, back to his big empty house.

Kidd and Zoe started for the door.

"What now?" Zoe whispered once they were in the hallway. "Do we think that—?"

"I don't know what I think," Kidd whispered back. "But it seems a little bit weird, doesn't it? He starts asking questions about The Grinning Murders last week, this week a body shows up."

"Might be a coincidence?"

Kidd raised an eyebrow at Zoe. "Might be a copycat killer, DS Sanchez."

Kidd reached out a hand and grabbed the door handle. He pulled it down hard and the flashing began almost instantly. Maybe they'd seen the shadows behind the glass and readied themselves for whoever was stepping outside. If Kidd had epilepsy, he would have been fucked. The flashing was relentless, he couldn't see a single one of their faces.

"They've got nothing to write about," Zoe said to him quietly. "You'll be a footnote on page six, don't worry about it."

"I'm not worried about that, I'm worried for my fucking corneas!" Kidd growled. "Jesus Christ!"

The flashing stopped after a moment and Kidd did his best to get his bearings. The vultures knew they weren't getting any meat off these two and they seemed to die down. Kidd wondered how much time they spent out here, whether it was just during the day or if they spent their nights out here too, waiting for Colin to leave, waiting to harass him. They must have cost the papers a fortune.

And then he caught sight of Joe Warrington at the edge of the pack. He was staring directly at the two of them, a shit-eating grin on his face. It took all of Kidd's willpower not to stick his middle finger up at him, but that would cause more trouble than it was worth. These local rags probably didn't have a damn thing to put on their front pages, a bobby behaving badly would make a decent headline.

Instead, he marched towards him.

Warrington looked a little bit frightened. After two encounters where Kidd hadn't wanted anything to do with him, having the DI suddenly coming at him was a bit much.

He stepped backwards. Kidd picked up the pace, taking his hands out of his coat pockets and pumping them at his side.

"Kidd, what are you doing?" Zoe asked beside him.

"Going to give an exclusive to Joe Warrington," he grumbled.

"Kidd, don't do anything daft."

"Oi! Joe!" Kidd shouted. "Can I have a word?"

At that, Joe Warrington broke into a run, almost stumbling over his feet as he took off onto the pavement. He barged past the waiting reporters and photographers and shot off into the fading light of Lower Teddington Road, but Kidd wasn't about to give up so easily.

He shrugged his coat off his shoulders and broke into a run after him, not about to let the little prick get away. His feet pounded against the pavement, kicking up gravel and dirt, his arms pumping hard at his sides as he tried to get control of his breathing. This was always easier when he was out running in the morning, usually a light jog rather than a sprint to catch a potential killer on a Thursday night.

He could hear Zoe shouting after him, but he ignored it, knowing that he was gaining ground on Warrington. He got closer to the lad and managed to grab hold of his arm, yanking him back so he was a little off-balance. Joe cried out.

"Joe Warrington, I'm arresting you for the—"

CRACK!

Kidd hadn't been expecting the impact as Joe Warrington's free elbow connected with his nose. Kidd threw his head back, his eyes watering, blood pouring from his nostrils. He collapsed to his knees, winded, unable to see anything, but able to hear the sound of Warrington's footsteps as they ran off into the night.

"Shit."

CHAPTER
NINETEEN

"What the fuck did I say to you?" Zoe asked as she got into the car next to Kidd. He'd taken off his tie and bundled it up to stem the flow of blood coming from his nose.

DS Sanchez had reached him in good time, stopping when she saw that Kidd was doubled up on the ground. She'd stared down at him, disapproval written so clearly across her face it might as well have been written there in Sharpie. He'd messed up, and he'd messed up big time.

First thing to do when you catch somebody is to restrain both their hands. He'd grabbed one and got elbowed in the nose because he didn't think Warrington had it in him to fight back. Now he was paying the price.

"I told you not to do anything daft, and what did you do?"

"Something daft," Kidd grumbled. He pulled on his

seatbelt and waited for Zoe to start the car, but she didn't. "Can we go? There are people looking."

"You mean you're not so photo-ready with dried blood on your chin?" she snapped. "Honestly, Kidd, did you forget how to be a police officer while you were off?"

"I was off for six months, I wasn't meant to do anything police-related or police adjacent. I was supposed to be de-stressing."

"Well, you've stressed me out, so maybe we should trade places," Zoe growled, starting the engine and speeding off into the night.

They'd not spent a huge amount of time at Colin's house, but the nights drew in pretty quickly in the winter and it was already dark. But it was only as they were driving, that Kidd realised they weren't going back to the station.

"Wrong turning, Zoe," Kidd said. She didn't respond, her eyes fixed on the road, her knuckles white where they gripped the steering wheel. "Zoe?"

"I'm taking you to the hospital, you complete idiot," she grumbled.

"What? Why?" Kidd growled. "We need to get back to the station."

"We need to get you checked over by a doctor."

"Zoe, I'm not—"

"Weaver left me in charge of you," she interrupted. "And if I don't take you to the hospital and something happens, like you pass out or don't show up for work tomorrow, it's my head in the smasher."

"Zoe, it doesn't hurt, I don't need to—"

"You're going and that's the end of it," Zoe snapped. "I don't want to hear another word. Just try not to bleed on the car because if you do, you're paying to have it professionally cleaned."

Kidd opened his mouth to respond but knew it would be no use. Zoe was very much in the driver's seat in every sense of the word. He had to do as he was told this time.

Kingston Hospital wasn't the usual madhouse that it could be of an evening. It had taken them a little while to get there because of traffic, and by the time they got seen to, the workday was practically over, much to Kidd's frustration. No more progress was likely to be made today.

A black male nurse took Kidd through to be checked over, making sure his nose wasn't broken, that he wasn't concussed. He cleaned Kidd up, getting any dried blood off his face, assessing any damage. Ben needed to put ice on it, which Zoe assured him they would do, and he needed to rest, something Kidd assured the nurse he didn't have time for, and they left.

As they made it back to the station, it already looked a heck of a lot quieter than it had when they'd gone to Colin's, and he anticipated the rest of the team would have been told to pack up and leave by Weaver by now. Kidd cursed the wasted time. Every second counted in a case like this, and he'd wasted precious seconds because of what happened with Warrington.

"What the bloody hell have you done to yourself?"

Diane squawked from behind the front desk. "You're back for half a day and you're already in the wars."

"Don't know what I'm going to do with him, Diane," Zoe said as she buzzed herself through the door. "Might have to lock him up myself, might be the only way to stop him bruising that pretty little face of his."

"You need to take better care of yourself!" she called after them. "I've just refilled the first aid kit, there should be antiseptic wipes in there!"

"Thanks, Diane!" Kidd called back, putting his hands in his pockets, only to find his blood-soaked tie in there. "Gross," he muttered. The whole thing wet through with blood, probably ruined. It was only a cheap tie anyhow, and no point mourning the loss of a piece of fabric. He shoved it back into his trouser pocket where his hand brushed against something solid that stabbed at his fingers.

He pulled out the small, white card that John had given him at the pub the night before.

God, was that really only last night? he thought as he fingered the delicate piece of card. It had crumpled a little at the corners, a little bit of his blood staining it, but all the information was still there, John McAdams, his phone number, email address…

"What's that?" Zoe asked as they walked.

"Nothing," Kidd said, crushing the card in his fist and continuing at her side.

He was about to head back to the Incident Room when Zoe grabbed him by the arm and dragged him into the canteen. Canteen was a little bit generous. It was a room with a couple of kettles and a couple of microwaves in it, definitely not a canteen and more of a staff room. There were some sofas dotted about and a couple of tables and chairs where people could eat if they weren't eating at their desk, which was pretty rare.

"We've got work to do," Kidd grumbled as Zoe sat him down on one of the chairs. "I don't have time to—"

"You still have dried blood on your face, Kidd," Zoe interrupted as she headed to the cupboard and pulled out the first aid kit Diane had told them about. She turned back to look at him. "And a cut on your nose. You're not walking back into that Incident Room and making DC Powell piss himself because you look like you've been a victim of a violent attack."

Kidd stifled a laugh and sat back in the chair. There was no arguing with Zoe Sanchez, that much was for sure. She brought over the antiseptic wipe and dumped something heavy and covered in ice in front of him.

"What on earth is that?"

Zoe shrugged. "Frozen Mac and Cheese."

"I'm not hungry."

Zoe snorted. "Good thing. It went out of date six months ago," she said. "When you've got yourself cleaned up, you should put it on your nose. For the swelling."

Kidd raised an eyebrow at her.

Zoe shrugged. "The nurse said ice, this is the best I can do unless you just want to stick your whole face in the freezer."

Kidd took out his phone, using the front-facing

camera to clean up. He really did look a sight even after what the nurse had managed to do for him. At least his nose wasn't broken. He cleaned the rest of the blood off his face and stared at himself. He didn't look quite as exhausted as he felt, so there was that at least.

"You look fine, Ben," Zoe grumbled. "Put the cold thing on your face now please."

"It feels fine, *Doctor* Sanchez."

"Just do it." She groaned. "I've had enough of fighting with you today, just put the ready meal on your face, the bruising is already coming through. It will just help."

Kidd grumbled and leant forward on the table, pressing the ready meal on his nose. He winced at the contact. Zoe scoffed.

"Doesn't hurt, my arse," she said, which made Kidd smile. "So, what the hell happened?" she asked. "I tell you not to do something daft, you chase Joe Warrington down the street, next thing I know you're crumpled on the ground with a nose bleed."

Kidd groaned and shook his head. "I grabbed his arm to arrest him, started saying the old spiel, then Joe swung back and cracked me in the nose with his elbow."

"Christ."

"I know," Kidd grumbled. "Should have grabbed both hands."

"Probably."

"Couldn't catch him," Kidd said. "He might look like a stick but he can motor when he needs to, lucky for him. I wasn't fit enough to keep up. All that running still hasn't done me much good."

"If you're about to go off on one about not being as young as you used to be, I swear *I'll* elbow you in the nose, and I'll actually finish the job and break it," Zoe said, looking Kidd dead in the eyes. She was kidding, trying to lighten the mood. "You're out of practice. It happens to the best of us."

"But he got away," Kidd said, taking the ready meal off his face. Zoe signalled for him to return it to his nose immediately, which he begrudgingly did. Another wince. "Who knows what he could be doing right now."

"Probably hiding somewhere because you've scared the shit out of him," Zoe said, taking a breath. "It's fine, Kidd, misses happen."

"Yes, they do, but what if Joe is the guy we're looking for?"

"Then we'll find him."

Kidd growled. "It's not that simple," he said. "We don't have a whole lot to go on, and if Joe is the guy we're looking for then he could be planning his next attack." He sighed and took the ready meal off his face, looking Zoe in the eyes. "The sooner we get that list from Belmarsh the better, that might give us someone else to go on."

"You say we've not got a lot to go on, Ben, but we have leads," Zoe said. "Don't look at me like that. We've managed to do a heck of a lot considering you've been on the case for one day. We're looking for the CCTV of the creepy old park ranger, we've got information from the people who found the body in the first place, and we have a potential suspect in Joe Warrington. It's been productive, Kidd, you've got to stop killing yourself about this."

When Zoe put it like that, it certainly sounded like more. There were leads, just nothing concrete. Then again, it had only been one day. He was just worried. The longer they left it, the less information they had, the more likely they were to find another body. And Kidd didn't want that on his conscience, not again.

"We need to keep an eye on Colin," Kidd said. "I don't like those reporters camping outside his house. I don't want him to do anything stupid."

"Are you counting him out?" Zoe asked.

Kidd shook his head. "Not entirely. It doesn't seem likely at this point, but I have to keep him as a suspect just in case he's managing to pull the wool over our eyes just like his father used to."

"And what about Joe?"

Kidd took a breath. "I saw the lad and I jumped," Kidd said. "It might be him, it feels like it could be, considering the level of interest he had in Colin and the original case, but that's not enough to convict him."

"So, you want to arrest him?"

Kidd nodded. "We'll arrest him tomorrow. I'll brief the team on everything that's happened, and if Weaver thinks it's the right call, we'll arrest him. Who knows what else might have come up while we were out."

They stayed there for a moment longer, Kidd resting the ready meal on his nose until all it felt like it was doing was making his face wet. He sighed and sank into his chair.

"What?" Zoe said.

"Just exhausted," he said. "It's been a day. I'm not used to doing all this anymore. Six months off and I'm screwed."

"Going out for drinks with your sister last night probably didn't help that, huh?" Zoe said.

Kidd chuckled. "That honestly feels like a decade ago."

Zoe stood up. "You done with that ready meal?"

"Yeah, why? You hungry?"

"Gross, throw it out," she said. "And let's get out of here."

"But the case—"

"Will still be here in the morning," Zoe interrupted. "Everybody else has gone home, I checked with Weaver while you were lusting after the nurse. He wants you here bright and early tomorrow morning so we can keep going."

Kidd sighed. He wanted to keep going. Even if he wasn't onto something right now, it was much better to feel like you're doing something rather than twiddling your thumbs. But Zoe wouldn't let him stay, that much he knew.

"Alright then," Kidd conceded. "An early night for me it is."

Zoe laughed. "No, I don't think so, You owe me a drink."

CHAPTER
TWENTY

Kidd failed to see quite how he owed Zoe a drink. She reasoned that she'd taken him to hospital and taken care of him while he was wounded. Kidd, on the other hand, thought that was bullshit.

"Okay, how about the fact that you disappeared off the face of the earth for six months and ignored all of my calls?" she asked. And that was enough to make Kidd shut his mouth and walk to the pub with her.

They found a quiet table in a corner, away from the dirty old men who seemed to basically live there—Kidd was sure he'd seen at least half of them there last night—and the prying eyes of any onlookers. Kidd's face wasn't looking great, bruises in full bloom where Joe's elbow had connected. It hurt to breathe, which couldn't be a good sign.

Kidd bought the first round along with a couple of plates of chips to share, hoping that might placate Zoe and at least go some way to making up for the fact he had gone totally AWOL and then proceeded to act like a dick on his first day back.

"Do you reckon it was Warrington?" Kidd asked eventually, having to raise his voice over the din.

Zoe shook her head.

"You don't?"

"No, that wasn't my answer," Zoe said. "That was me shaking my head to us spending the whole day working only to spend the whole evening talking about work." She took a sip of her pint and seemed to relax into her chair almost instantly. "I don't want to talk about it."

"Doesn't it stay in your head though?" Kidd asked. "Something like this is so... I don't know, it's not exactly ordinary. I can't get it out of my head."

"Well, Kylie Minogue," Zoe said with a lazy smile. "That would be why *you* got signed off for six months because of stress and I stayed in the job."

"Harsh."

"But true," she said. "You have to learn to let go. You've got to leave the job behind when the door closes, otherwise, you'll just be sending yourself into an early grave."

Kidd shrugged. "Old habits die hard."

"And you'll die harder if you're not careful," she said. "Life is stressful enough without carrying the weight of your work around with you too."

Kidd took a sip of his drink, knowing in his heart of

hearts that she was right. It was what Liz had been telling him just yesterday, and he would need to take it on board before it ended up killing him. How many sleepless nights had he had since he joined the Met? How many more could his body take?

"You don't want to talk about work, what do you want to talk about?" Kidd asked. "How are things with you? You still with that fella…" he trailed off, scrabbling for the name.

"Mark?" Zoe winced. "No. He broke up with me a couple of months back."

"Oh shit, I'm sorry, Zoe, I didn't know."

"You would have if you'd picked up your phone," she said with a wink. "I'm not too cut up about it now. I was then, we'd been together for over a year."

'Did you think he was the one?"

Zoe shook her head. "I think I knew he wasn't right for me. It was just easier to ignore it and have somebody, than be alone."

"Oh, you want to talk about being alone? I know an awful lot about being alone." Kidd laughed. "But I'm sorry it didn't work out. That sucks. And I'm sorry I vanished for so long. I think…" he trailed off, finding his bearings. "I think I needed to vanish a little bit, get away from it all."

"I understand that."

"I just felt like the best way to do that was to cut myself off from it entirely," he said. "Not see anybody, not talk to anybody remotely attached to the job."

"Now, I don't understand that so much," Zoe said. "I'm your friend, Ben. Friends first, colleagues second. I wouldn't want to sit around with you and talk about work the whole time we were together, that would be boring as shit. I just wanted to know how you were, how you were getting on being off work. Friend shit, not work shit."

"Okay," Kidd said. "I'm sorry. It was just my way of coping."

"And how did that work out for you?" Zoe asked.

Kidd sighed. "Terribly. I spent most of the time trying to distract myself by reading or watching TV, running or going to the gym, all things that failed. Except the running, I got into running."

"Still can't catch up to a young man though."

"Wow, alright, a bit too soon, you can see the bruise on my face but the one on my ego is way bigger!" Kidd said with a smile. "And the rest of it was just... empty days I guess. I saw a lot of really nice places around the area, I took a solo trip out to Germany for a while, I saw a fair bit of Liz and the kids but..."

"But you were thinking about work the whole time?" Zoe suggested. Kidd shook his head. "Craig, then."

And there was the kicker. So many people knew about Craig, he'd been such a huge part of Kidd's life, he came up way more often in conversation than he would have liked. But talking about it with Zoe was different. As she'd already said, they were friends first, colleagues second. He could bring down that guard a little with her. At least, he felt like he could.

"Are you still looking for him?" Zoe asked.

Kidd shrugged. "On and off. The trip to Germany was retracing our steps a little bit from our holiday there."

"Why?"

"To torture myself, I think?" Kidd laughed. He didn't want to tell her everything that had happened in Germany. That he didn't only retrace their steps but when to city after city looking for him, falling into all sorts of trouble that would certainly make her look at him differently. He didn't want to dwell on it if he could help it. He shook his head and looked up at her. "Or maybe just to remember the last time we were both truly happy. That's probably what it is."

"Oh, Ben—"

"I know, I know, it's pathetic."

"It's not pathetic," Zoe said. "If he knew you were looking for him—"

"He'd probably call me pathetic," Kidd interrupted. He knew he would. Craig was like that. "It's been two years."

"Do you think he's…? I don't know how to ask this, Ben."

"Do I think he's still alive?" Kidd finished. Zoe nodded.

Kidd never knew the answer to that question. There were times when he thought that Craig was alive, like he would know somehow if he was really gone for good. It was what kept him looking, checking missing persons reports to see if anything had shown up. It was what made him go to Germany. It was what made him talk to anyone who would listen, and even to people who wouldn't. But there were other times when he thought he had to be dead. Because if he was alive, why the hell wouldn't he come back? That was a door Kidd didn't want to open.

"I want to believe that he's alive," Kidd said. "But believing he's alive means accepting the fact that he doesn't want me to find him. Probably."

"So will you just keep on looking?"

Kidd shrugged. "Maybe. The trail is ice cold, frozen over, but I still hold out hope that he'll just walk back into my life one day."

"And what will you say to him?" Zoe asked.

Kidd laughed. "I'd probably punch him, then kiss him, then yell at him."

"He'd deserve that," Zoe said. "Do you miss him?"

Kidd took a sip of his drink. "All the time," he said when he'd swallowed. "Work is a good distraction."

"The last six months must have been hell for that."

"Oh, you better believe it," Kidd said.

The chips arrived and Zoe smothered hers in salt and vinegar, putting a large glob of mayo on the side of her plate. She dove in with full force. She really must have been hungry. It was only when Kidd had the first bite that he realised he was too. He'd been running on fumes.

That's why I couldn't catch the kid, he thought. *I was under-fuelled.* He knew it was wishful thinking, but he'd take it.

"What about Facebook?" Zoe asked.

Kidd felt like he'd missed a step somewhere. Maybe he'd been so engrossed in the chips she'd been talking to him the entire time and he hadn't noticed.

"Huh?"

"In looking for Craig," Zoe said. "You've checked it, right?"

"Of course," Kidd replied. "He was never really big on it. He never got the whole social media thing. He'd get tagged in photos and stuff, but he'd never do anything himself."

"And that's remained totally empty?"

"Not a thing," Kidd said. He checked Craig's page pretty often, gotten lost in some of their old pictures. He'd lost hours to that during his leave.

"What about his friends?"

"What about them?"

"Well, he had friends besides you, right?"

"Yeah," Kidd said. "He had a whole work life and stuff. Why?"

"Well, check there maybe?" Zoe said. "His friends will know who you are. If he's just gone off-grid, maybe one of them has an idea where he might be."

"I don't know," Kidd said. It was one thing for him to still be living in a world where Craig hadn't left him, but to dredge up those feelings in other people just felt harsh somehow. Also, given how their relationship had been towards the end, he couldn't imagine they'd be thrilled to hear from him.

"I do," Zoe said. "You've got nothing to lose, right?"

"My dignity?"

Zoe shrugged. "You got beaten by a foetus in a foot race, Ben, you don't have any of that left."

CHAPTER
TWENTY-ONE

The conversation switched from Craig to other men in Kidd's life, a conversation that was mercifully short because... well... since Craig, there hadn't been anyone else in Kidd's life. Any energy he had for a romantic relationship had been dedicated to looking for Craig, something that made Zoe give him those sad puppy dog eyes.

"What about the guy with the card?"

"What guy with the card?" Kidd asked.

Zoe rolled her eyes. "You're not as sneaky as you think you are, Benjamin Kidd," she said. "You had a card in your pocket and you were looking at it all goo-goo eyed after we got back from the hospital. Where did that come from?"

"It came from a guy who gave it to me last night," Kidd said. "But I wasn't interested, so I declined."

'But you kept his card," Zoe said.

"Yeah—"

"Well, you can't have been that uninterested if you held onto his card," Zoe said. "And the way you were looking at it, I would say you were far from uninterested. I would even go so far as to say you were interested."

"Oh, would you look at the time," Kidd said. "I really must be going."

"Okay, okay, okay, I'll stop," Zoe said. "One more drink?"

It didn't take much to twist Kidd's arm. Just like things had been last night with Liz, it was nice to be out of the house, nice to be talking to someone other than himself.

They nursed another drink for an hour or so, Zoe's soft because she was driving, Kidd enjoying a second pint, chatting until neither of them could stand to be awake any longer, and they parted ways, Kidd experiencing tipsy déjà vu as he left the Druids Head.

"I can give you a lift home?" Zoe offered once they were outside. "It's on the way, it's no bother."

"I'll be fine," Kidd said. "Could do with the fresh air."

"Lightweight!" she called after him as he set off in the direction of home.

"See you tomorrow!" he called back.

He took a different route, wandering back towards the river and enjoying the quietness of it. In the distance, he could hear the music pumping out from one of the restaurants along the riverfront, the occasional sound of a car revving its nuts off across Kingston Bridge.

He found himself fondling John's card in his pocket again. Would it hurt to call him? Or just to message him? They could go for a drink. He could test the waters, see if he was interested.

If you're thinking about it, you're probably interested, he thought. He knew Zoe was right. He hadn't thrown the card away. He was in denial.

His phone buzzed in his pocket and he took it out, seeing a message from Liz.

> Hope you had a good first day back.
> Tilly says Hi, Tiny Tim says *blows raspberry noise*

Kidd laughed in spite of himself.

> I say hello and *raspberry noise* back.

> Today was fine.

> Just getting back into the swing of things.

She didn't need the gory details of the day. If she was already worrying about him, hearing he'd had his nose smashed in and ended up in hospital was hardly going to help that. He pocketed his phone and kept walking, wrapping his jacket around himself to battle against the wind coming in off the river. He passed the restaurants, a couple of people sat outside eating and smoking, definitely out of their minds given the state of the weather, but who was he to judge?

He continued down beneath the bridge. Someone barged into his shoulder. He hadn't even noticed anybody there, he'd thought he was alone.

Then the punch came, straight to the ribs, enough to knock the wind out of him. He stumbled backwards, lifting his arms to protect his face. Kidd wasn't much of a fighter, but he'd been in his fair share of scuffles since he'd joined the Met and he knew how to defend himself. He just wasn't expecting to have to do it now.

He was disorientated, someone wearing dark clothes, a hood pulled up far enough that the lights cast shadows on his face, shadows that made him impossible to identify.

The assailant swung a punch that Kidd blocked, knocking it out of the way with his forearm before launching an attack of his own. He swung his fist towards their stomach, connecting hard. He heard a low grunt as he stumbled backwards, falling over his own feet, and hitting the ground hard. But he wouldn't be deterred. He looked like he was about to go for Kidd again as he dragged himself to his feet.

"I wouldn't," Kidd said, drawing himself up to his full height, not letting the sharp stab of pain in his side make him wince. He still had his fists raised and he darted towards the man, but the guy broke into a run, heading off down the river and out of sight.

Kidd immediately ran after him, right back the way he'd come, along the river, past the people eating in restaurants. He was tall, quite slender and when his hood fell back Ben hoped he'd be able to make out something of his face but got nothing. He wasn't catching him. There was no way.

Kidd slowed down to a stop, leaning on a nearby railing to steady himself. His side already hurt from where he'd been caught by surprise, the running hadn't helped.

"Twice in one day," he grumbled. "Can't make a habit of this, I'll fall apart."

He watched the younger man running away, back in the direction of the Druids Head. His gait was strange, like he wasn't trying to put weight on one of his legs as he ran. Ben wondered if he'd known he was there, had he been watching him the entire time?

He took a few deep breaths before straightening up and starting back towards his house. Not how he thought his night was going to end, that much was for certain.

Kidd walked away from the river, back through town, and out the other side, a little more vigilant of anyone who might be watching him. He kept his coat pulled tightly about him, his collar up high, just in case whoever it was had a change of heart and wanted to come back and try again. He could only hope he'd decided to go home and nurse the bruise Kidd had given him.

He cradled his fist in his hand. He'd definitely caught something hard, either a nose or a cheekbone, because his hand ached. He'd have to ice it when he got in.

The house was cold, colder than it had been the night before. Kidd threw the lights on and hung his coat by the door, locking and deadbolting the door behind him. It was quiet. On any other day, Kidd wouldn't think twice about the quiet, but getting jumped had set the wind up him a little. He tried to shake it off, but there was a feeling of being watched creeping across the back of his neck and he couldn't make it leave.

"Stupid," he said, walking from the hallway into the kitchen. He turned the lights on in there too, half expecting to see someone stood there waiting for him, waiting to finish the job, but found he was alone. Just as he had been for the past three years. Now, there was a bleak thought he could definitely do without.

He headed upstairs and grabbed his laptop, bringing it downstairs and setting it on the dining table. He boiled the kettle and made himself a cup of tea, setting himself up with a bag of frozen peas in a tea towel to ease the ache in his right hand.

Zoe had given him an idea, enough of an idea that instead of going to bed and getting a decent night's rest before having to go back to hunting down Jennifer Berry's killer tomorrow, he was trawling through Craig's social media profiles. Even as he did it, he felt wrong, like he was spying on somebody, looking at something he shouldn't have been looking at.

He checked the tagged photos, where there were photos of him and Craig together, their holiday in Germany, their holidays across other parts of Europe, cosy nights in and ridiculous nights out. He fell down a rabbit hole of memories that culminated in Craig's friends, seeing if any one of them had a recent photo with him, wondering which one to reach out to, if any.

He landed on Craig's sister, Andrea. They had been fairly close. In fact it had been Andrea who had told him that Craig had gone missing. It seemed like she was also the last person in that family who still believed Craig was alive.

He started to type out a message to her, trying not to be too maudlin, trying to make it seem that it was more for a catch up than it was for anything else but he didn't quite know who he was trying to fool. He asked her if she had seen him, or if she too had given up looking for him like everybody else.

He read it back and pressed send, staring at the screen as the message vanished, the little tick sitting next to it to show it had been delivered. He debated watching it to see if it was enough of an enticement to bring her online. But that just felt too sad, even for him.

Kidd downed his cup of tea and sat back in the chair. He caught sight of his reflection in the mirror, of the state that Joe Warrington had made to his face. It would only look worse in the morning.

And then another thought crossed his mind.

He started to search for Joe Warrington. Nothing had been put up since earlier that day, rumours and conjecture about what was going on, about how the police were handling it. It was enough to make Kidd want to reply, or at least to tell him that he was wrong, but he knew it wouldn't do any good.

He found his way to Joe's Instagram and started to scroll through it. It was mostly pictures of Joe with minor celebrities, at crime scenes every now and again, the captions often reading BREAKING NEWS and wanting people to go to a link in his bio.

But then Kidd saw something that made his blood run cold. There was a picture of Joe Warrington standing next to one of their witnesses, Lydia Coles, the two of them mid-laugh, a candid photo of the two of them looking stupidly joyful some two months ago.

Every person that Hansen killed was someone known to him.

If that's the pattern he's following, Lydia could be in trouble, and they needed to act fast.

CHAPTER
TWENTY-TWO

He fished his keys out of his pocket on his way to the door, the jangling was too loud, ripping through his head in a way he hadn't anticipated. He felt light-headed from the run, his stomach hurting where he'd been hit, his ankle still giving him trouble even after all these weeks. He shouldn't have been running, but he had to. He hadn't expected the old DI to have anything in him, not after what he'd seen.

The house was deathly quiet. Something he was glad of. He quietly closed the door, not wanting to wake anyone else up, and snuck upstairs.

His heart was still pounding even as he made his way into his room. He shut the door, throwing off his hoodie and pressing a hand to his side. He winced as a stab of pain rushed through his body.

"Jesus," he grunted. He pulled the knife from the waistband of his joggers. He hadn't planned to use it, that was what he told himself, he only planned to have it just in case.

Just in case what?

He didn't know the answer to that question.

There was a stirring along the landing. He froze, staring at the door, half expecting it to open, for someone to come in and tell him that he'd been found out.

But nothing came and he exhaled.

The DI was making him skittish. He was chomping at his heels, getting closer to finding him out, and he couldn't let that happen. Action needed to be taken. And it needed to be taken now.

He waited for the house to go quiet, tucked the knife back in his waistband, and left.

CHAPTER
TWENTY-THREE

K idd woke up late, a lot later than planned, but his social media rabbit hole had taken him into the wee small hours and he couldn't bring himself to get out of bed. Hardly the best start to the day.

He drove to the station, parking up next to Zoe despite all the spare spaces because he knew it would piss her off. Just a little game to play.

"What on earth happened to your face?" Diane exclaimed as he walked through the front door. There were a couple of people waiting on the chairs opposite the front desk who looked up in alarm, one of them wincing as they caught sight of Kidd. He looked at his reflection in one of the windows. He hadn't thought it looked too bad, all things considered.

"I got elbowed," Kidd said. "Remember? I came in looking a wreck with DS Sanchez, blood everywhere."

"I remember," Diane said with a roll of her eyes. "I

just didn't think it would look this bad. Should you be here?"

Kidd laughed. "I've got to be, Diane. You know me, no rest for the wicked."

"No rest, period," she corrected. "You work too hard."

"Got to keep the old brain ticking over somehow," he said. "Have a good day!"

He beeped himself through the door and headed straight for the Incident Room, surprised to see that DC Campbell and DC Ravel had already arrived.

"You're early!" Kidd said as he walked in the door, hanging his coat up. "Something wrong?"

"Yeah," Campbell said. "There's a killer on the loose, don't you—" he stopped as he looked at Kidd and took in the state of his face. "What happened to you?"

"A child beat him up," Zoe said from her desk. She was shovelling a croissant into her mouth like she hadn't eaten in a week.

"It wasn't a child," Kidd corrected. "We went to see Colin Hansen last night and when I tried to grab hold of Joe Warrington to bring him in for questioning, he swung back and elbowed me in the nose."

"So *that's* why you didn't come back," Campbell said, leaning in a little closer. "Christ, he really did a number on you. Proper got you."

Kidd shrugged. "Yeah, I know, it bloody hurt," he said. "Zoe had me go to the hospital. Did you find out much about Jennifer Berry?"

Campbell quietened down, opening his mouth to speak before stopping himself.

"What?" Kidd asked.

"The dad didn't take it well, sir," Campbell said. "Properly broke down. Family liaison is going there again this morning to try and keep him together."

"Reckon he's up to be questioned?"

"I'd say no, sir."

Kidd shook his head. "Not the answer I'm looking for, Campbell, want to try again."

"If you're sensitive, sir."

"I'm always sensitive, Campbell. I'm not you," Kidd said.

"What are we doing about Warrington?" Zoe asked, dumping her croissant packet and coffee cup into the bin. She wiped the crumbs from her mouth as he approached. "He still your prime suspect?"

"Wait, when did he become the prime suspect?"

"Keep up, Campbell," Zoe said, with a wink. "We went to see Colin Hansen last night, turns out the kid has been asking him a lot of questions about the murders over the past couple of weeks. Now he's using it for leverage on his social media sites and things, but before that, he wanted a lot of detail from Hansen."

"So, you think he's our guy?" Campbell asked.

"And there's one more thing," Kidd said. "I was doing a little bit of digging on Joe's social media last night—"

"After we left?" Zoe interrupted. "Kidd, take a fucking night off, Jesus!"

"Look, it helped alright?" he snapped. "There's a picture of Joe and Lydia together, all smiles, acting foolish, and now I'm pretty worried about her. Campbell, I emailed you a link to the post, can you get it printed and up on the board."

DC Campbell walked away and started tapping away at his computer, the printer kicking into life and spitting out the photo that Kidd had found himself staring at last night. He looked at it carefully, at their smiling faces, at Lydia who had seemed so frightened when they'd gone to see her yesterday.

"You think she's in danger?" Zoe asked quietly.

Kidd nodded. "I'm hoping she isn't, but if Joe is our guy, the pattern that Hansen followed was people that he knew. Maybe he knew Jennifer too. I'm hoping I can find that out today."

"What do you want us to do about Joe?" Campbell asked, reappearing at Kidd's side.

"I want a team to go and arrest him this morning," Kidd said. "If we can pull up his records and get there ASAP, that would be great. Bring him in for questioning, hopefully, we can get this thing wrapped up by lunchtime, sound good?"

"Sir?" DC Ravel piped up from behind her computer. "Might want to hold fire on that."

Kidd looked sharply over at DC Ravel who gestured for him to come closer. Kidd did just that, Campbell and Zoe following close behind, all crowding around Ravel's computer. She clicked on a few emails and a video popped up.

It was grainy, dark footage with a timestamp in the corner, Monday night at around 2300.

"The footage is taken from a block of flats opposite one of the gates," Ravel said. "You know who that is right?"

Kidd looked a little closer. It wasn't the best footage in the world, but he could take a wild stab. An older man took a set of keys out of his pocket and started fiddling about with the lock on the gate, looking nervously about himself before heading inside.

"Is that—?"

"The night watch ranger, Evan Petersen?" Ravel finished. "I believe so, sir," she added. "It's from Monday night, fits with the time that Jennifer Berry was killed. Why on earth would he be going back into the park after hours?"

"And why didn't he tell us about that in the first place?" Kidd added. He was getting sick of people not giving him the full story when asked. "Great work, Ravel. We should bring him in for questioning. But we should still grab Joe Warrington just in case." Kidd could feel himself getting excited. They were getting closer, he could feel it. "We get anything else come in I should know about?"

The door to the Incident Room flew open, Weaver blowing in, his phone held aloft in his hand.

"What the bloody hell is this?" he barked, his Scottish accent filling the entire room. Campbell winced next to Kidd and scurried away, not wanting to get caught in the crossfire. "I come into the office to find this sent to me, the force's Twitter getting tagged in all sorts of shit. What the hell are you playing at, Kidd?"

Ben walked over to the DCI, taking the phone off him, and watching the video being played out. It was from yesterday evening. It showed Kidd running towards Joe and Joe running away, stopping at the moment when Kidd grabbed Joe's wrist, Joe complaining of the pain before the video cut out.

"Where's the rest of it?" Kidd asked.

"What are you talking about?" Weaver asked, his face suddenly adjusting as he noticed the state of Kidd's face. "What happened to your face, son?"

"Joe Warrington happened to my face, boss," Kidd replied. "The part of that video that's missing is the part where he swung back and clocked me on the nose with his elbow."

"Y'alright?"

"Fine, sir, went to hospital, wrote it up, all sorts, but that part of the video is missing," Kidd protested. "It's not as cut and dried as me trying to grab hold of the lad. I wanted to bring him in for questioning."

"What?"

"Had a lead from Colin Hansen, sir, and he ran off," Kidd said. "Can we respond to this? Can we tell people that he assaulted a police officer?"

Weaver puffed out his cheeks. "Not likely. Not the way we do things, I'm afraid."

"What? So he gets to say what he likes about me and I can't respond?" Kidd said. "You should see his social media channels, sir, it's all propaganda and fake news. He's just stirring up trouble."

"Can't arrest someone for that, Kidd," Weaver said. "If you could, half the government would be in jail cells."

"Still, we need to go and get him today, bring him in for questioning," Kidd said. "And DC Ravel is going to go and bring in Evan Petersen, too."

"The old park ranger?" Weaver looked confused. "You think you're getting closer to figuring this out, Kidd?"

Kidd shrugged. "We're certainly doing our best, sir."

Weaver nodded. "Glad to hear it."

Without another word, he left, passing DC Powell in the doorway, leaving the young boy looking a little dazed and confused.

"What have I missed?" Powell asked.

"Keep your coat on, Powell," Kidd said. "We've got work to do."

CHAPTER
TWENTY-FOUR

K idd had barely given DC Powell a moment to get settled before they were back out of the door and on their way to Jennifer Berry's house. He'd sent DS Sanchez off to arrest Joe, and DC Ravel with DC Campbell to pick up Evan Peterson. Even though it was nice to have someone in the office to hold the fort should anything come up, all of them being out on the case felt good, it felt like they were doing something and progress was being made.

DC Powell hung on for dear life as Kidd swung the car around the corner and parked it up outside Jennifer's house. There was another car here, one that he knew belonged to Caitlyn Jones, the FLO on the case. If the state of Jennifer's father was even close to what Campbell had said, it was going to be difficult to get a lot out of him. But they needed to at least try. He'd tread carefully.

He got out of the car, DC Powell following suit,

looking nervous and a little bit cold stood outside the semi-detached house. If he'd been looking up the case files for The Grinning Murders, then he'd know this house pretty well. Much like Colin, the Berrys hadn't moved since it all happened. So it was the same house that Kidd had been at many years ago, just with the slightest facelift. Someone had taken up gardening. It scrubbed up well.

"You alright?" Kidd asked.

"Yeah, course," DC Powell replied. "He was just in quite a state yesterday. Caitlyn did a wonderful job of calming him down, but he was devastated."

Kidd could only imagine. It had happened twice in his lifetime, to two of his loved ones. It didn't bear thinking about.

"We'll try and keep it brief," Kidd said. "And you have to give me a nudge if you think I'm going in a bit hard."

"Right."

"That's DS Sanchez's job normally, so now is the time to show if you can fill her shoes," Kidd said with a wink. DC Powell smiled and nodded before they started towards the door. They sidled around the Range Rover parked on the driveway to the porch where Kidd rapped on the door twice.

"Bit harsh, sir," DC Powell said, a smile tugging at the corners of his mouth.

"Yeah, you're going to fit in with us just fine, Powell," Kidd said with a grin, quickly rearranging his face to something a little more solemn as the door opened.

Caitlyn Jones opened the door, her porcelain face slipping from a smile to a look of surprise when she saw Kidd.

"What did you do?"

"To my face? Yeah, it's a long story," Kidd said. "Good to see you, Caitlyn, it's been a while."

"Well, some of us had a six month work holiday," she said with a smirk.

"And which one of us was that?"

"Oh, neither one of us, Kidd, just making conversation," she replied. She lowered her voice and leaned in a little. "You might want to tread a little carefully here. He's fragile, which I'm sure you understand, but I thought you might want a warning." She looked over at DC Powell. "Hey, DC Powell."

"Hey, Caitlyn."

"Come on in, wipe your feet," she said, stepping back into the house and standing by the door waiting for them to comply. Kidd made sure to wipe his feet, Caitlyn's eyes on him the entire time. She was deadly serious, apparently.

Kidd walked in and was taken to the living room where a man was sitting in an armchair, staring at the TV screen. They were reporting what had happened to his daughter—thankfully, without any of the detail—and asking anyone who had any information to contact the police. DC Campbell must have put it out yesterday, as soon as they'd found out who it was. He might have been a bit of a dickhead, but there were certainly times when he knew how to do his bloody job.

"Mr Berry?" Kidd said stood in the doorway looking over at the gentleman. He looked so similar to how he'd looked all those years ago when Angela had been taken away from him. The only thing that had changed, was that his formerly black hair was now dotted with specks of grey and he'd grown a beard. His skin looked paler though, more sickly. Kidd could understand why.

He looked over at DI Kidd and DC Powell, his face shifting in acknowledgement, a thin-lipped smile that told more of how he was feeling than words ever could. They were stood there staring at a man who had been shattered almost beyond repair. How he was still even able to function was beyond Kidd.

"I hope you don't mind me stopping by," Kidd said as he walked further into the living room. "I don't know if you remember me, I worked on Angela's case. You probably don't."

Mr Berry shook his head. "I'm sorry, I don't. But thank you for catching him. Though, maybe I shouldn't be thanking you, I don't know. Did you even get the right man?"

"I'm sorry?"

"It's happened again," he said, gesturing at the TV where a picture of Jennifer filled the screen. Tears filled his eyes. Maybe this hadn't been such a good idea. "Did you catch the right man if it's happened to my little girl too?" He choked at the end of the sentence and Caitlyn grabbed the box of tissues from the cabinet and passed them to him. He took one and balanced the box on the arm of the chair.

"Would anyone like a spot of tea?" Caitlyn asked. "I know I could do with one, I'm gasping."

"I can make it," Mr Berry said.

"No, no, Mr Berry, I know where the things are," she said. "DI Kidd? DC Powell?"

"Yes, please," Kidd said. "Just a splash of milk."

"Same for me, with two sugars," DC Powell said, offering her a soft smile. "Do you want me to give you hand?"

"DI Kidd?" Caitlyn asked.

"Off you pop, DC Powell, I'll be alright," Kidd said. He waited as DC Powell left the room, but he turned around to catch Kidd's eye as he reached the doorway. He gave him a thumbs up. Kidd had to stop himself from rolling his eyes. "I just wanted to ask you a couple of questions about Jennifer—"

"Jenny," Mr Berry corrected. "We always called her Jenny. It's weird to hear people calling her Jennifer all the time. Sure, it's the name we gave her when she was born, but it's not what we called her. It was always Jenny."

"Jenny, then," Kidd said. "I just wanted to know a little bit more about her, what she studied at university, the people she spent time with. The better picture we can get of her and what her movements might have been around the time of the murder, the better chance we have of catching whoever it is that's behind this."

"Right, right, right," Mr Berry said, trailing off, not

managing to tear his eyes away from the screen. They stayed in silence for a few more seconds, until the news item moved on and they started talking about some politician's latest mishap. Mr Berry turned his attention to DI Kidd. It was only then that Kidd noticed the dark circles beneath his eyes. He can't have slept much last night. How could he?

"So just a few quick questions, Mr Berry," DI Kidd said. "Then we'll get out of your hair." Kidd cleared his throat. "I'd love to get a sense of Jenny's movements leading up to the incident," Kidd continued. "Anything you can give us."

"Well, she attends Kingston University," Mr Berry started. "So she left in the morning for a day of classes. I understood that she was going to be going out later with a few friends from one of her courses."

"What was she studying?"

"Drama," Mr Berry said. "So she was going out with some of her acting friends, I think. But she mentioned she was doing a short film and, forgive me, there's been so much going on, my brain's in a muddle."

"That's okay, Mr Berry, take your time," Kidd said, taking a few quick notes.

"She was doing a short film, linking up with a couple of people who were studying screenwriting, or film, so I think maybe that was happening on Monday and they were going out afterwards," Mr Berry said. "I'm sorry, I'm not being very helpful."

"You're being a lot more helpful than you think, Mr Berry, I assure you," Kidd said, offering a smile.

"Tea?" Caitlyn shuffled back into the room with two mugs in her hand, one for Mr Berry, one for herself. DC Powell followed close behind, handing a mug to Kidd and placing his own on a coaster by the sofa.

"Thank you," Kidd said, taking a quick sip of the tea before returning his attention to Mr Berry. "Do you know who the film was with?"

"I'm sorry," Mr Berry said, seeming to slump even further in his chair. "She never said. I probably should have asked."

"What about the people she spent her time with at university?" Kidd asked. "Who were her friends there?"

Mr Berry was clearly racking his brains to find a name, any name, but he seemed to be drawing a blank. "Lydia," he said suddenly.

Kidd sat up sharply. "Surname?"

"Not sure on a surname," Mr Berry said. "But she had a friend called Lydia she would stay with on occasion. I think they met at Freshers because they weren't on the same course, you see?"

"Yes, I do," Kidd said, his brain suddenly going at a million miles a minute. Lydia found the body. If she found the body, there was no chance in hell she wouldn't recognise her, was there? Or was there? The pictures had been pretty messed up. Jennifer Berry had been through some major trauma before the body was found, and all that blood… was Kidd making excuses? Or had he misjudged Lydia entirely?

He turned his attention back to Mr Berry and put a smile on his face. "Thank you so much for your help, Mr

Berry," Kidd said. "We won't take up any more of your time." He took a big gulp of his tea before getting to his feet.

They said their goodbyes to Mr Berry and started towards the door. Caitlyn touched Kidd on the shoulder before he left.

"Thank you for going easy on him," she said. "I can't imagine this is easy for you either."

Kidd forced a smile. "I'm doing alright," he said. "Got to keep chugging along, eh?"

"You take care of yourself," she said. "And if you need me, you know where I am."

They left the house and walked back to DI Kidd's car.

"Poor guy," Powell said. "Must be awful for him having to go through all of that again. Can't imagine what that must be like."

Kidd nodded. "I know," Kidd replied, pulling out his phone. "Just going to call DS Sanchez, give me a second."

"Sure thing, boss," DC Powell said, getting into the passenger's seat.

The phone only rang twice before Zoe picked up. "Yeah?"

"Lydia Coles knew Jennifer Berry," Kidd said flatly.

"Shitting hell."

"I know."

"So, now you're drawing a line from Joe Warrington all the way to Lydia Coles?" she asked. "Do you think she was involved?"

Kidd shook his head. "I'm not sure. Jennifer was pretty unrecognisable when she was found, I don't want to automatically believe the worst here," he said. "But I still think Lydia might be in danger."

"Right," Zoe said. The silence on the other end of the line was enough to make Kidd nervous.

"What's happening, Zoe, you've gone quiet on me?"

"I'm outside the university now," she said. "Joe Warrington is missing."

CHAPTER
TWENTY-FIVE

Kidd had quizzed Zoe on the phone, asking where Joe was and what on earth she meant by missing.

"Went to his house and he wasn't there, dad claimed to have not seen him for a day or so, has a brother who hasn't seen him, mum was suspiciously quiet," she said.

"Under the thumb?"

"Almost certainly," she said. "So I came to the university, been to reception and he hasn't signed in to any of his classes today. He's gone off-grid."

"Because he knows we're after him," Kidd said, cursing how impulsive he'd acted last night. If he'd have played it a little cooler they wouldn't be in this situation in the first place. "Fuck."

"Going to head back to the station now," she said. "How did it go with Mr Berry?"

"The only information I got was that Lydia and Jenny

were friends, but it's enough to give us somewhere to go, I guess," Kidd said. "I'll see you back at the station."

————

Kidd drove back to the station with enough speed to have DC Powell looking a little green by the time they got there. He stayed outside for a moment longer to get some air while Kidd headed inside.

"Got a message for you," Diane said from the front desk, putting her finger up to him so he would wait, which he did gladly. "Had a phone call from a Colin Hansen."

That caused Kidd's ears to perk up a little. "What did he say?" he asked.

"He mentioned you went to see him last night, he's been getting *hounded* by the press, his exact words, that's a quote," she said. "They're encroaching on his driveway now and he's getting worried. He can't sleep. He's just..." she sighed. "He's having a really tough time of it, the poor lamb. I stayed on the phone with him for a little while, managed to calm him down, but I wonder if it's worth popping round to see him again?"

Kidd smiled at her. She was a good egg, Diane. The Met was a better place for her being on it.

"I'll look into it, Di, thank you," he said, beeping himself through the door and heading back to the Incident Room. DS Sanchez and DC Ravel were already there, both huddled around Ravel's computer as she likely added notes to the case file.

"Just got a message off Diane at the front desk," Kidd said as he approached the computer. "The press is hounding Colin Hansen."

Zoe rolled her eyes. "Fucking vultures."

"Yeah," Kidd said. "I don't know what he wants us to do. We can get them to go away, but they're only going to come right back. Does that make them vultures or cockroaches?"

"Vicious hybrid," Zoe said. "We have to do something. We can't just leave him." She sighed. "I mean, if it wasn't enough that this was being brought back into the light, he's having to deal with all of that. He can't even go to work."

"Okay," Kidd said. "I'll send a couple of DC's later on to do a drive-by, disperse anyone still there, make sure he's alright. How does that sound?"

"It sounds like you're doing the bare minimum," Zoe said. "But we've got a murderer to find."

Kidd shrugged. "My thoughts exactly. So, Joe wasn't there this morning? What were you saying about his dad?"

Zoe groaned. "A total dickhead." Serious hatred for the police. Thinks we're the scum of the Earth and didn't want to help."

"Really?"

"Monosyllabic answers from start to finish."

"But mum seemed…"

"She seemed like she had something to say but didn't dare say it in front of Mr Warrington," Zoe said with a sigh. "I just felt sorry for her. He was one of those people who somehow managed to manspread across an entire room. The worst."

"Can we get her to come in, do you think?"

Zoe shrugged. "I can make a call," she said. "No guarantees though. Mr Warrington is retired, so he's home a lot."

Kidd took a breath and headed back towards the board. DC Ravel appeared at his side.

"I've got printouts for the board, sir," she said, handing him a stack of photos. She'd printed more photos she'd found on Joe's Instagram of him and Lydia together. It made Ben feel nervous all over again. If his inkling was right, Lydia could be next on his list and that meant trouble. There was too much pointing to him.

"Thank you, Janya," he said. "Anything from Belmarsh yet?"

"Nothing, sir," she said. "Happy to chase though."

"That would be great, thank you."

"One last thing," she said. "I've been in touch with the Anders family. Everyone's present and accounted for."

"So Jennifer Berry is a horrible coincidence?" Kidd said, looking over at DS Sanchez for confirmation. She shrugged.

"Sorry, sir," DC Ravel said. "But at least it's just one body…" she trailed off and headed back to her desk, that familiar clacking returning to underscore the tension in the room.

Kidd sighed. *It's just one body, for now,* he thought.

"DS Sanchez," Kidd called out as he stuck the pictures on the big board.

"Yes?"

"Can you go and check on Lydia for me?" he asked, still looking at the board, at her smiling face next to Joe's. Was that the face of a killer? Kidd didn't know, but what other leads did they have at this point? "I'm worried. If she knew Jennifer and is also friends with Joe, she could be—"

"No problem," she said. "Leave it with me."

"Thank you."

The door to the Incident Room opened, DC Campbell appearing in the frame looking incredibly pleased with himself. Zoe looked him up and down and walked away. She wasn't having any of it, leaving it to Kidd to figure out what had him preening like a bloody peacock.

"Evan Petersen is here," Campbell announced. "And he's ready for the interview."

CHAPTER
TWENTY-SIX

K idd gathered himself and took DC Campbell with him to the interview room. He'd done interviews with DC Campbell in the past and he tended to be a little bit jumpy, thinking he was a detective on a TV drama rather than in real life, but that had been well over six months ago, maybe he had grown up a little. Though, recent experience told him that was wishful thinking on his part.

Kidd walked into the interview room to find Evan Petersen already sat with his lawyer at his side. He'd expected the old man to bring a lawyer, even though he wasn't technically under arrest. It made him seem more guilty of something, sure, but Kidd wasn't about to tell anybody that.

"Good afternoon, Mr Petersen, lovely to see you again," Kidd said. "How are you?"

"I'd be much better if I wasn't here," he said.

"Ain't that the truth," Campbell said. Kidd shot him a look and he seemed to wince under the pressure of it.

"I don't believe we've met," Kidd said to the lawyer, a middle-aged man with grey, flyaway hairs dancing at his temples. He reached out a hand. "DI Kidd."

"Matthew Michaels," the man replied, taking Kidd's hand and shaking it. "My client is quite distressed by all this."

"Me too," Kidd said. "Quite a gruesome murder, wasn't it? A good reason to be distressed, I'd say."

Campbell cleared his throat and took a seat, Kidd followed suit, offering Mr Petersen a smile that he didn'treturn. This man was grumpy through and through. Now that they were all sat at the table, the room seemed even cosier than it had done a few moments ago. He was almost touching knees with Evan and the walls seemed to be pulling in closer. Kidd hated the interview rooms. They were claustrophobic and always ended up getting too hot, especially in the summer months. But usually, it was enough to unnerve whoever was being questioned.

He focused his gaze on Evan Petersen, trying to get a read on him. For being "distressed," he looked remarkably calm. Although, Kidd suspected he was more like a duck on water, calm and collected on the face of it, legs swimming at an alarming rate underneath.

"Mr Petersen, I take it DC Campbell told you why you're here?"

"He mentioned something about asking me a few questions," Evan said, his voice as gravelly as it had been last time Kidd had spoken to him. Kidd was fairly sure that Campbell would have said something a little more detailed than that, but if Mr Petersen was going to act like a fool, Kidd was going to treat him like one.

"Well, Mr Petersen, here is the situation," Kidd said, "we've had a brutal murder occur on this borough, a woman was attacked, and then, once dead, her corpse was mutilated to replicate a set of murders that originally occurred fifteen years ago. I asked you a few questions just yesterday, in fact, about your whereabouts over the past couple of days, and it turns out, there was a rather huge detail that you left out, wasn't there?"

"I don't know what—"

"Okay, let me rephrase that, there *was* a rather huge detail that you left out. There's no denying it, Mr Petersen, and leaving it out only leads me to believe that you might be hiding something else. Are you hiding something else, Mr Petersen?"

"No."

"Well, then why keep it from us?"

Mr Petersen clamped his mouth shut and looked to his lawyer for support. Kidd waited for whatever wisdom he was going to come out with. When nothing was forthcoming, he decided to carry on.

"Let me take you back to Monday night, shall I, Mr Petersen?" Kidd said. "You left work as you usually do, locking the gate behind you at 10:30 pm, is that right?"

"Yes."

"And then you proceeded to, I don't know, go home to a loved one, maybe carrying a guilty conscience—"

"DI Kidd, I hardly think that's appropriate," the lawyer finally chimed in.

"Fine," Kidd said. "But you went home and then, some thirty minutes later, you decided to go back out again. And you unlocked the gates to the park and went inside, not coming out again for a solid hour." Kidd looked over at Mr Petersen who was shifting uncomfortably in his seat. "I think you know what my next question is going to be, Mr Petersen."

He didn't say a word. He stared at DI Kidd from across the table, his grey eyes not giving away a single thing. Kidd shook his head.

"What were you doing going into Bushy Park in the middle of the night, Mr Petersen?" Kidd asked. "It's a very simple question, and if you have nothing to hide—"

"Don't push it, DI Kidd," Mr Michaels said.

"I'll push it as far as I want to."

"Am I under arrest?" Mr Petersen asked, the slightest shake in his voice.

Kidd sighed. "No, Mr Petersen, you're not under arrest, but if you can't give me a straight answer to these questions—"

"I'd left something behind."

"What?"

"My anniversary gift for my wife!" he barked. Kidd backed off, leaning back in his chair, waiting for him to elaborate. "Monday was our anniversary, fiftieth if you must know, and my wife was already furious I'd been working and then even more furious because I told her

I'd left the gift at work. Things haven't been good for us recently. We've been having troubles. I don't want to lose her after all these years, DI Kidd, so I went back to pick it up because I didn't want her to be upset with me."

Kidd took a breath, exhaled. "Can your wife confirm this?"

"Absolutely," Mr Petersen said. "I can give you her phone number, you could call her right now, she'll happily tell you what a forgetful klutz I am."

Kidd allowed a smile to tug at the corners of his mouth. "Well, a belated Happy Anniversary to you both," Kidd said.

"Am I free to go?" Mr Petersen asked, looking at the door like he was about to burst through it and leave a Mr Petersen shaped hole in it if Kidd said yes.

"Just a few more questions, while I have you," DI Kidd said. "I want to know the kind of people that have been hanging around Bushy Park the past week or so."

Evan sat back in his chair, his tension in his bony shoulders seeming to slough off. He was no longer under suspicion for murder, it was hardly surprising that he'd relaxed.

"Parents and their children," Mr Petersen said, not looking at Kidd, trying to think. "Old couples, a lot of old people."

"Anything out of the ordinary," Kidd said. "You mentioned briefly about how frustrated you get at some of the people who spend their time in Bushy Park, what kinds of people are they?"

Mr Petersen let out a heavy breath, practically a

groan. "University students mostly, like I said," he said. "They dress so scruffily, make a whole lot of noise, and leave a mess everywhere."

"Is that out of the ordinary?"

"Not really, unfortunately," Mr Petersen said. "We've had a few complaints coming in over the last week or so about some of them."

"Really?" Kidd said. "What about?"

Mr Petersen rolled his eyes. "It was nothing really. Young people being entitled. They were filming something, a short film or something. They got antsy and started trying to get the parents to quieten their kids down. The parents got upset, told us, but by the time we got to them they were long gone."

"How many of them?"

"Just two," Mr Petersen said.

"Description?"

"A girl with long brown hair," Mr Petersen said. "And a boy with dark curls, that's about all we got."

CHAPTER
TWENTY-SEVEN

D S Zoe Sanchez left the office around the same time as Kidd, grabbing her coat and heading out to her car. The picture of Lydia with Joe Warrington that was now stuck to the board was burned into her memory. Knowing that Lydia knew Jennifer Berry too, made it even the worse. Too many times in her career she'd seen vulnerable young women be left at the mercy of asshole men, and she wanted to do everything in her power to protect her. So maybe on the drive there, she broke the speed limit a few times. So long as no one saw, it was okay.

She pulled up outside the dilapidated old house, taking a deep breath before heading down the ramshackle garden path to the front door. It really was a hole. She would have hated to live here as a student. In fairness, her digs when she'd been studying hadn't been much better, but as an adult the thought of living here made her skin crawl.

She knocked on the door, ignoring the flaking of the paint as she did so.

No answer.

She knocked a little harder, the glass shaking in the windowpane and making a hollow sound that echoed right down to Zoe's bones. She stepped back and looked up at the house. There were a couple of lights on the upper floor. Either they were burning electricity or they just hadn't heard her.

She went back to the car, switched it on, and pressed down on the horn, long and hard.

A face appeared at a high window. She gestured emphatically to the door and the face disappeared at breakneck speed.

"At least that got their attention," she grumbled, heading back down the path.

The door opened before she reached it, TJ Bell stood bathed in the yellow light of the hallway, wearing a pair of jeans and a different baggy hoodie. His gormless face stared out at her, clearly confused as to why she was there. It made her want to yell.

"Can I come in?" she asked, though it wasn't so much a question as it was a demand. It was fucking freezing.

"Yeah, yeah, sure," he grumbled, opening the door to the porch and letting her in. Zoe had half hoped for heat to rush out and greet her, like it did whenever she went back to her parents' house, but instead, she was met with that same cold damp that had enveloped her when she'd come here yesterday. How they could live like this was beyond her.

"I was going to come and change my statement," he babbled. "I just haven't had a chance to do it yet. I had a class late yesterday afternoon so couldn't do it then and today... I just haven't done it yet."

"You're alright," Zoe said, holding out her hands in a calming gesture. "I'm not here about that. I'm here to see Lydia."

"She's not here," TJ said with that same drawl that seemed to accompany everything he said, like even talking was too much effort. Their entire conversation could have been finished a heck of a lot faster if he talked at a semi-regular speed.

Zoe waited for him to elaborate, but nothing came. "Can I ask where she is?"

"Erm," TJ looked off towards the wall and thought about it. Zoe was so close to punching him. "Not sure."

"When did you last see her?"

"Erm—"

"No, TJ, no 'erm', tell me when you last saw Lydia Coles, please."

"Yesterday," he said. "I said my goodbyes after you guys left, went to my class, and she was out when I got back."

"Did she come home last night?"

"Erm-"

"TJ!"

"I don't know, I was tired," he babbled. "It had been a long day, I didn't know if—"

"Did you think to check on her at all?"

"She has other friends, and I think I heard her go out this morn—"

"You think?" Zoe was getting frustrated. She needed a straight answer and TJ wasn't giving her anything close to that. Every sentence started with an 'erm' and he didn't seem to realise quite how severe the situation was. He'd seen the body, hadn't he? Was he just not affected by any of this?

"We live with three other people," TJ said. "It could have been any of them."

"Would she have gone out with Joe Warrington?"

"Who?"

"Christ, never mind," Zoe grumbled.

Kidd was going to flip out. Zoe could already see that he was on edge. Everything that was happening was already hitting a little too close to home with how the case went down the first time and the last thing he wanted to do is end up with another body. If it ended up being Lydia he'd never forgive himself.

"Can you call her?"

"Erm—"

"TJ," Zoe said firmly. "I need you to call her, call her now."

Zoe waited as TJ fumbled in his pocket and took out his phone. A few taps later and he held the phone to his ear. Zoe could hear it ringing from where she stood, the steady beeps that were making her heart run a little faster the longer they went on.

The line went dead.

"Can you try again?" Zoe asked.

"Do I need to be worried?" TJ asked, his face shifting from one of gormless indifference to one that actually looked scared for his friend. "Like, do I need to be worried about Lydia?"

"The honest answer to that is, I don't know," Zoe said. "We hope not. We're just trying to figure out where she is. She might be in trouble."

"Oh shit," TJ said, tapping his phone again and putting it to his ear.

The line rang for a few moments, moments that seemed to draw on for hours in Zoe's mind before the line went dead once again. Her blood ran cold.

"Do you mind if I take the number?" Zoe asked. TJ waited while Zoe tapped it out into her phone. "I'm going to give you my number and you need to call me if you manage to reach her. Oh, and if you could ask your housemates if they've seen her since yesterday afternoon, that would be great."

Zoe gave him her number and turned to leave.

"DS Sanchez," he called after her. Zoe was already halfway out the door, but turned to look at him bathed in the light of the lone, naked bulb in the hallway. "Is Lydia going to be alright?"

And it was in that moment she felt sorry for TJ. He was living in this house, probably miles away from his family and one of his friends had gone missing. Sure, he was a little slow to help her but it's probably a lot for anyone to deal with.

"We're going to do our best to bring her back in one

piece," Zoe said, forcing a smile onto her face. "She could be on her way home from class right now, for all we know. Just keep me posted, yeah?"

TJ nodded and Zoe walked away, already dialling Kidd's number.

CHAPTER
TWENTY-EIGHT

I t wasn't confirmation that Joe Warrington was there, it was barely a confirmation of ID, but the description was enough. Kidd knew it was a long shot to get the parents to come in and confirm anything, the people that had complained. No doubt they would have made the complaint and then promptly forgotten all about it, not knowing that in just a few days a girl they now knew to be Jennifer Berry was going to show up dead.

"Maybe some of them would recognise her," Campbell reasoned. "She was beautiful, how could you forget a face like that?"

"Mostly because those parents weren't likely thinking with their dicks, DC Campbell." Kidd groaned as they walked back to the Incident Room.

Kidd had let Mr Petersen go, apologising for any distress they'd caused and thanking him for his time. But really, all that they'd accomplished was to tighten the ball that had formed in his gut and make his sense of urgency to find Joe Warrington all the more pressing.

"You want me to get confirmation on the anniversary, sir?" DC Campbell asked.

"That would be great, thank you, DC Campbell," Kidd replied.

He walked over to his computer and logged in for the first time since he'd returned to the force. Just as he had done on his computer at home the night before, he started to look at Joe Warrington's social media, desperately looking for a clue as to where he might be.

The last thing that he'd posted was the video of DI Kidd grabbing hold of his arm. It had gone a bit viral, with enough people tagging the Met Police and asking them what on earth they were going to do about this brutality for it to gain some traction. Kidd ignored it and kept scrolling, looking for anything that would give him a lead.

His phone rang next to him, buzzing loudly on the desk and drawing the attention of DC Ravel and DC Powell from behind their desks. Kidd held up a hand in apology and picked his phone up, seeing DS Sanchez's name across the screen. He answered quickly.

"Hello?"

"I was trying to call you a second ago," she said. "It went to voicemail." Kidd could hear the sound of traffic around her and figured she was already been on her way back.

"I was in an interview," Kidd said. "What have you got for me?"

"Nothing good I'm afraid," she replied. She told him about her conversation with TJ Bell, how he hadn't seen Lydia since they'd been there yesterday afternoon and that he was going to keep her updated. It was enough to have DI Kidd sitting back in his chair, worried.

"That's not good."

"I know."

Kidd sighed, his voice crackling against the receiver. "Thanks, Zoe. Get back here as quick as you can."

"Nearly there," she said.

As he hung up the phone DC Powell looked up from behind his computer screen. "Developments, sir?"

"Lydia Coles hasn't been seen since yesterday afternoon," he announced to the room. "I need someone checking her social media, someone to call the university, DC Powell, can you—?"

"On it, sir."

"DC Ravel—"

"Pulling up her social media now, sir," she said.

"Anything for me to do, sir?" DC Campbell asked.

"Yes," Kidd said. DC Campbell looked like he was about to burst with the anticipation of it all. "If you can find where DS Sanchez got the good coffee yesterday, that would be amazing, I'm absolutely gasping."

DC Campbell visibly deflated and then left the room.

Kidd turned back to his computer and continued looking through Joe's social media. It felt like he was missing something, something that had been right in front of his face. He could mentally cross Evan Petersen off his suspect list now. The only lead he had was Joe

Warrington, and if he was totally honest with himself, Colin Hansen.

He didn't want to believe it was Colin. After everything he'd been through, that was the last thing he wanted to think. But he couldn't count him out yet, not until he had confirmation from Belmarsh that he hadn't been there, that his story checked out.

Joe was a different story. Colin had said Joe was asking an awful lot of questions. That was either a journalist's—or apparently a filmmaker's—morbid fascination, or it was him scouting for tips. If Joe was already out and about last night, it also tracked that he could've been the one who'd attacked him by the river. If Joe wanted to scare him off because he was getting too close, then that tracked too.

The door to the Incident Room opened and Zoe breezed inside, heading straight over to Kidd's desk. She looked worried. Kidd imagined he was reflecting the same thing back at her.

"What's the next move?" she asked.

"I've got DC Ravel looking up her social media to see if she's been online and DC Powell is calling the university to see if she's been there," he said. "Other than putting a callout on official channels to see if anyone has seen her, I'm not sure what to do."

"We can't be sure when she was last seen," DS Sanchez said. "We'll have to wait."

"If we wait too long it might be too late."

The door to the Incident Room opened again, more

furiously this time, DC Campbell marching back into the room at breakneck speed, a panicked look on his face.

Kidd looked at him, noticing the missing coffee cups in his hands. He really did look freaked.

"What?" Kidd said, resisting the urge to roll his eyes. What was he playing at? "It's just coffee, Campbell, Jesus, there's no need to get in a state about it."

"No, it's not that," Campbell said. "It's Diane, sir."

Kidd narrowed his eyes. "What about her?"

"She just came to get me," Campbell said. "There's someone at the front desk who wants to talk to you. Goes by the name of Warrington."

CHAPTER
TWENTY-NINE

Kidd felt his stomach drop. It all felt a little bit too easy. DC Campbell looked panicked and Zoe was staring daggers into the side of his head. If looks could kill.

"He wouldn't," Zoe said flatly. "There has to be some mistake."

Campbell shrugged.

"Might need more than a shrug, DC Campbell," Zoe snapped.

"Diane didn't give me anything more," DC Campbell replied. "Just said there was someone called Warrington at the front desk and she seemed distressed."

The words snagged on DI Kidd's brain. "Wait a minute, she?"

"Yes," DC Campbell replied.

DI Kidd nodded. "Thank you, Campbell, now please go and find that coffee, I have a feeling I'm going to need it."

Kidd walked out of the Incident Room, closely followed by Zoe, no doubt keen to see exactly what was going on. When they made it out to the reception area, there was only a woman standing there. She was short, her dyed brown hair a little grey at the root cut into a bob, a nervous smile drifting across her face as the two officers locked eyes on her.

Her hands were placed in front of her, she was practically wringing them. Her eyes darted to the door as if considering a quick getaway, and then back to Kidd and Zoe.

"Mrs Warrington!" Zoe exclaimed, her face bursting into a smile and walked over to greet her. DI Kidd, on the other hand, turned to Diane with a questioning look. She lifted an eyebrow and shrugged. It seemed she didn't know why Mrs Warrington had decided to come here either. They'd have to hear it straight from the horse's mouth, as it were.

Zoe walked over to Kidd who was still waiting by the door, ushering the incredibly nervous Mrs Warrington forward. She looked like she might burst into tears at any moment.

"Mrs Warrington just had a couple of things to tell us," Zoe said with a soft smile. "You got a few minutes to take her through and have a chat?" she asked, widening her eyes when Mrs Warrington wasn't looking. Kidd had a sneaking suspicion this was going to be good.

"Diane, do we—?"

"Interview Room Three is free," she said. "Do you

want a cuppa, my love?" Diane asked with a smile. "You look like you could do with one, it's glacial outside."

Mrs Warrington smiled, seeming to relax a little. "That would be lovely, thank you."

Kidd and Zoe took Mrs Warrington through to Interview Room Three, Kidd silently hoping that the darkly painted walls and claustrophobic nature of the room wouldn't put her off whatever it was she was about to tell them. Zoe opted to sit with Mrs Warrington, DI Kidd taking one of the seats opposite. At least that way it wouldn't look like an interrogation.

Diane popped in and dropped off a cup of tea in a polystyrene cup for Mrs Warrington. She wrapped her hands around it and held it close. It stopped her from wringing them for a few moments, and she looked a few shades calmer than she'd done out in the reception.

"So, Mrs Warrington," Kidd started. "I understand DS Sanchez went to see you earlier on today. Is everything okay?"

"I'm not under arrest, am I?" she asked suddenly. "I don't want any trouble, just…" she trailed off, her eyes finding the bubbles at the top of her tea and focussing on them with such intensity you'd be forgiven for thinking she was trying to part it like the Red Sea.

"It's okay, Mrs Warrington," Zoe said softly. "This isn't an interview, we're not recording anything, none of this is going to be used against you. This is just a chat. You wanted to come in and talk to us, so… whenever you're ready." Mrs Warrington turned to face Zoe, her face lighting up a little bit at her kind nature. She really was good at the human interaction part of all this. While Kidd had a tendency to fly off the handle if he felt like someone was withholding information, Zoe knew exactly how to get them to talk.

"I don't really think it's anything," Mrs Warrington said. "But Philip, you met my husband, Philip. He didn't want to give anything away. He's... funny with the police."

"I heard," Kidd said, trying to keep the icy tone of derision out of his voice and likely not succeeding by the way Zoe turned her head to glare at him.

"Well, he said that he hadn't seen Joe for a day or so," she said. "The truth is, we've not seen Joe for a couple of weeks now." She was struggling to hold it together, that much Kidd could see. The combination of her son being missing and seemingly betraying her husband tumbling down on her all at once. "I was starting to get worried, but he was answering texts and phone calls, so I assumed he was just busy with school. He stays in a house nearer to the university, wanted to have the full experience." She shook her head. "I know it's probably nothing, but I wanted to say more than what Philip said. It didn't seem right to keep it from you, especially if he might be in trouble." She looked from Zoe to DI Kidd, her eyes a little glassy, tears already forming and threatening to break the dams of her eyelids and cascade down her already red face. "Is he, Detective? Is he in some kind of trouble?"

DI Kidd looked to Zoe and then back to Mrs Warrington. He took a breath, knowing that, in some ways, this was a sink or swim moment. He didn't want to panic her any more than she already was, but maybe this would help get them a little more information or at least some insight into the kind of boy Joe was. It could help.

"We wanted to speak to Joe about a murder investigation," DI Kidd said flatly. "He's been reporting on it on his social media channels, and we know that he knew both the victim and someone else who is now missing." He cleared his throat. "I don't want to worry you, Mrs Warrington, but I do want you to know just how important it is that we find him."

"Oh my goodness," she gasped.

"We're not saying your son is responsible," DI Kidd said firmly. "But we want to find him, make sure he's okay. Rule him out if it's not him, do you understand?"

Mrs Warrington nodded, trying to compose herself. The importance of this seemed to weigh on her quite heavily, dragging her shoulders down and deepening the lines in her face.

"Do you have any idea as to where he might be?" Kidd asked. "Where we might find him? We've checked your house, we've checked with the university and no one seems to have any idea."

"I'm not sure," Mrs Warrington said. "Things changed after he moved out to go to university. He didn't come home as much, he became more private. If I ever tried to ask him anything, he'd get defensive. Philip told me not to worry about it, that he was just growing up and didn't need me coddling him all the time. So I tried to stop."

The tears broke free now and started to run down her face. Zoe, much better in these kinds of situations than Kidd, quickly wrapped an arm around the woman's shoulder and squeezed her tight. There was obviously a lot going on for her. A child fleeing the nest was just one part of it. She felt like she'd lost touch with him and now this...

"Mrs Warrington, I understand this must be very difficult for you," Kidd said. "But you understand the severity of the situation, yes?"

Mrs Warrington nodded.

"Good," he said, forcing a smile. "If you think of anything over the next day or so, anywhere he could be. Or if you hear anything, you just let me know, okay? I'll give you my card and you can call me whenever." He looked at her earnestly. "About this, or anything else happening at home, okay?"

Mrs Warrington considered him carefully. DI Kidd reached into his jacket pocket and took out a card, sliding it across the table to her. She hesitated at first, and Kidd wondered whether her husband was the kind of man who looked through her pockets, looked through her purse. But she took it and put it away.

"Thank you," she said quietly.

There was a knock at the interview room door, it opened to reveal DC Ravel who greeted them with a smile. She started when she saw Mrs Warrington, quickly shifting her focus to Kidd.

"Sir, I wondered if I could speak with you for a moment?" Her eyes darted to Mrs Warrington and back to Kidd again. "It won't take a second, if you're busy...?"

"No, no," DI Kidd said. "I think we're just about finished here." He turned his attention to Mrs Warrington one more time. "Thank you for your time, Mrs Warrington, I really appreciate it."

"My Joe is no killer," she blurted. "I know my boy and I know he's no murderer, he couldn't do that to those girls he just—" She gave a strangled cry as she started sobbing again.

"It's okay," DS Sanchez said softly. "No one is accusing him of that just now. We just want to get to the bottom of this." She looked up at Kidd. "You go, I'll be alright."

"Thank you again, Mrs Warrington."

CHAPTER
THIRTY

DI Kidd followed DC Ravel out into the corridor. A couple of uniformed officers squeezed by them, nodding at Kidd on the way past, DC Ravel was looking up at Kidd expectantly.

"What do you have for me?" he asked.

"I finally heard from Belmarsh, sir," she said.

"Great," Kidd said, his voice coming out a little louder than he was expecting. Finally, a little bit of progress on that front. Maybe it would give them a new lead. Having spoken to Mrs Warrington, there was a part of him that was hoping it wasn't Joe after all, even with all signs pointing to him. She already seemed devastated. "Do we need to go back to the Incident Room?"

"We can if you want, sir." She shrugged. "But it's a pretty easy list to reel off."

"How do you mean?"

"The only person that has gone to see Albert Hansen in prison is Colin," DC Ravel said. "Sometimes he would bring a guest, but every single name in the book for the last twelve months was Colin Hansen."

DI Kidd deflated. Could he have lied to them? Would he have? He'd seemed so skittish, so distressed when they'd gone to see him, could that all have been a ruse? Like father, like son?

He remembered all those years ago, how Albert had managed to convince them time and time again that it wasn't him, that the whole thing was cutting him up inside, when he was the one doing the cutting. It wasn't beyond the realm of possibility that Colin could be lying to them too.

Kidd sighed.

"Sorry, sir," DC Ravel said. "I wish I had better news."

"So do I," Kidd replied. "But no need to apologise. We just need to keep moving on."

"Oh, one other thing," she said. "Another little message from Diane, apparently Colin's been on the phone again. He's still not happy with having the press outside his house. Wants you to go and check it out."

"Me?"

DC Ravel shrugged. "That's what Diane said."

Kidd understood that. He'd been Colin's connection to the case all those years ago, a familiar face. He couldn't begrudge him that.

They walked back to the Incident Room, coming in to find that Campbell had tracked down some coffee—though, after a single sip it was clear that it wasn't the nectar of the gods that Zoe had given him yesterday—

and DC Powell was still glued to his computer. Both of them popped up like meerkats when he walked into the room.

"Anything?" Campbell asked.

"It was Mrs Warrington," Kidd said. "Joe's mother. It's been a couple of weeks since she last saw her son. So not *unhelpful*, but not exactly giving us much to go on either. Anything new here?"

"Still checking on Joe's social channels," DC Powell said. "Nothing since he posted the video of you chasing him before getting clonked in the face."

Kidd turned to him sharply and Powell visibly shrank at his desk.

"Campbell's words, sir, not mine."

DI Kidd swung round to Campbell who was smiling at him sheepishly. "Just a joke, DI Kidd," he said. "Harmless bit of fun."

Kidd raised an eyebrow. "Really?" he said. "Well, if you like, for a harmless bit of fun, how about you get clonked in the face by *my* elbow and we'll see if you're still smiling about it—"

"Got a sighting, sir!" DC Powell announced.

"Sorry?"

"Sighting of Joe Warrington outside his home," Powell said. "PCs were on their beat, wandering around the roads and such, and saw someone they thought looked familiar. Trying to get visual confirmation now."

"Fuck visual confirmation," Kidd said, already heading for the door. "Campbell, shift it. Where?"

Powell shouted the address out as Kidd and Campbell hustled to the door, nearly crashing into DS Sanchez in the doorframe.

"What's going on?" she asked, startled.

"Joe Warrington has been seen outside his house," Kidd said, breathlessly. "Going to go and pick him up. Maybe we can put an end to this before dinner."

"Fast work," she said.

"And we had another call from Colin complaining about the vulture/cockroach monsters outside his house," Kidd said. "Can someone go and check it out?"

"Happy to," Zoe said.

"How was Mrs Warrington?"

Zoe shrugged. "Shaken," she said simply. "But she'll be alright. She wants this over with as much as the rest of us do, I think."

Somehow Kidd doubted that. "We'll be back soon."

———

Kidd drove like a maniac to the address Powell had given him. Campbell was practically giddy in the passenger seat, Kidd having to stop himself from telling him to sit the fuck still or he'd crash the car on purpose.

They pulled onto the Warrington's street and slowed down a few clicks, the streetlamps on the road steadily clicking on, bathing the greying dusk with an orangey glow. There were a few people about, couples with dogs, older ladies and gentlemen wandering the streets, but Kidd didn't see Warrington.

He'd remember the smug little shit's face anywhere.

It was burned onto his retinas until he managed to catch him. They made it to the Warrington's house. There were a few lights on inside, a couple of shadows moving behind net curtains. Not enough to get confirmation of who was inside. There was no car here though, which meant Mrs Warrington hadn't made it home yet. That might make this a little easier.

Kidd got out of the car, Campbell quickly following suit, and made his way to the front door. The porch light switched on, sending a harsh white flood of light across the two of them, and apparently waking up the yappiest dog known to man. It practically screeched at them from behind the door.

"Christ, a little rat dog," Kidd grumbled. "What obsession do people have with tiny dogs that bark like that?"

He knocked on the door, his fist landing heavily and rattling the panes of glass. A light switched on inside, illuminating someone coming towards the door.

A man opened it. Tall with dark hair that was cropped close to his head. His face was fixed in a snarl the second he laid eyes on them, no doubt recognising Campbell from earlier in the day.

"What now?" he crowed. "Haven't you harassed my family enough? Isn't this is getting a little ridiculous? I'll report you, make a complaint. What's your badge number?"

"Believe me when I say that won't be necessary," Kidd said, forcing a smile onto his face.

"Dad, what's—?" Another person walked into the

well-lit hallway and promptly froze, his mouth hanging open in surprise. Apparently, Kidd's face wasn't one that was easy to forget either.

"Go back inside," Mr Warrington barked. "I'm handling this."

"Don't go anywhere," Kidd said before Joe could even so much as move. "You're under arrest."

CHAPTER
THIRTY-ONE

I t wasn't the smoothest arrest that Kidd had ever conducted. Mr Warrington wouldn't stop yelling as they arrested Joe, who was frighteningly calm as they escorted him out to the car. Mr Warrington was insistent that Joe didn't say a word until a lawyer was present, and once again, demanded both DI Kidd's and DC Campbell's badge numbers.

Joe didn't say a word. He followed them out to the car, his face remaining completely calm, completely unfazed by everything that was going on. It set Kidd on edge. This was what it had been like when they'd arrested Albert. He'd been so calm, so put together, like he'd been expecting to get caught. Or that he thought he could talk his way out of it, even if he'd been caught red-handed.

Joe hadn't been caught in the act. In fact, at this point, they had no concrete proof to tie him to the murder. But

Joe didn't know that. What else would they be arresting him for?

Now Kidd knew why Mrs Warrington had been so shaky, and what Zoe meant when she said Mr Warrington was an asshole. He was a Grade A dickhead. While his son was complying and doing as he was told, he wouldn't stop yelling. It only meant there were people out in the street watching everything happen, making the whole situation all the more embarrassing for him and his son.

At least Mrs Warrington didn't have to see it, Kidd thought.

They booked Joe in at the station and waited for his lawyer to arrive, Kidd preparing his questions, gathering the photos they had, any evidence that they could use. He was expecting a no comment interview, but he at least needed to try.

He wondered how Zoe was getting on.

CHAPTER
THIRTY-TWO

DS Zoe Sanchez left pretty soon after DI Kidd. DC Ravel had offered to come along with her but she was fairly sure it wasn't going to take all that long, and politely declined. If DI Kidd came back with Joe Warrington, he was going to need all the help he could get.

She got in her car and drove to Colin Hansen's house, getting caught in a little traffic on the way, but still making pretty good time. What surprised her, was when she pulled up outside the house to find that nobody was there.

She checked the address on her phone to make sure it was the right one and, sure enough, it was Colin's address alright, but any harassers that had been there earlier had since vanished. In fact, the entire house was dark. Not even the porch light was on.

Zoe took her phone out of her pocket and dialled

Colin's number. It rang for a while before it clicked off, asking her to leave a message.

"Hiya, Colin, it's DS Sanchez, we spoke yesterday," she said. "I was just responding to the call that you made earlier on today and again this afternoon about the press outside your house. I'm here now, if you wanted to speak to me at all. I'd love to make sure everything is okay before I head back to the station."

She hung up the phone, gave it a second and dialled one more time. Nothing. Just his voicemail again.

Zoe turned to look at the house again. There was a strange eeriness about it being completely pitch black while the rest of the street was lit up, either by porch lights or by the streetlamps.

She wondered if maybe the crowds had dispersed and he'd managed to get out for a little bit with his dog. He'd mentioned the dog not being able to be anywhere but the garden because he couldn't take him for walks. Maybe he'd taken him for a long walk.

But then, why the phone call? she thought.

Zoe got out of the car, pocketing her phone as she walked towards the door. The porch light clicked on illuminating the driveway, just as it had a night ago when she and Kidd had been here. She turned back to her car, half expecting the paparazzi to appear like they'd been lurking in the shadows waiting for him to come home or something. But there was nobody here. Maybe they knew something she didn't.

She reached up and knocked, only to find it open at her touch.

Odd, she thought.

She pushed it with the palm of her hand. The house was dark, quiet, the only sound the creak of the door as it steadily swung open.

Zoe inadvertently held her breath. Like if she made even the slightest sound, she would disturb whoever was in the house.

She looked back to see that Colin's car was there, still waiting on the driveway. Had he left the house and accidentally left the door unlocked? It was an easy mistake to make.

Zoe took out her phone and dialled DI Kidd's number. He didn't pick up. He was likely in an interview with Joe Warrington by now, not wanting to be disturbed. She stepped outside onto the drive to make the call, looking up at the darkened house, unable to keep the chill out of her bones.

"I've just got to Colin's property," she started, keeping her voice low. "It's Zoe, by the way. There's nobody here, no press, no nothing. They seem to have vanished into thin air. But, since I was here, I thought I'd check on Colin anyway, see if he was okay, but the house is empty and the door is unlatched. I'm calling you because I'm going in to check it out."

She kept the phone to her ear and stepped inside. She could hear her breathing distorting against the phone, coming back at her warm. Her footsteps seemed loud, like she was stomping her way into the hallway even though she was trying to keep her steps careful.

DS Sanchez cleared her throat.

"Hello? Colin?"

Nothing.

"This is DS Sanchez. Your front door was open."

She turned the corner into the living room and fumbled along the wall to find the light switch. She switched it on. And dropped her phone.

CHAPTER
THIRTY-THREE

Thankfully, Joe's lawyer didn't waste too much time getting there. Kidd had a sneaking suspicion that Mr Warrington would have had him on speed dial, prepared for just such an occasion. He seemed like the type.

Alyssa Johnstone wasn't someone that Kidd had encountered before, a younger woman with dead-straight black hair, the smoothest-looking brown skin he'd ever seen, and a soft expression. Though, Kidd refused to be fooled by such things, considering most lawyers liked to at least start with pleasantries before advising their client to give you shit during the interview.

They were in Interview Room One, the largest of the interview rooms at the station. The walls were painted dark, CCTV in every corner, the tape recorder primed and ready to hear whatever Joe had to say.

DI Kidd guided Joe and his lawyer into the room,

taking the seat across from them with DC Campbell at his side. He, again, seemed jittery, excited at the prospect of them getting their man. Kidd remained sceptical.

Kidd pressed the record button and proceeded with the formalities.

"My name is DI Kidd, this is DC Campbell who will be taking a few notes and presenting you with the evidence we've acquired so far," Kidd stated, turning his gaze to Joe who was still looking remarkably calm. No matter how much Kidd looked at him, he just couldn't read him, couldn't figure out what was going on inside his head. *Just like Albert,* he thought.

Alyssa cleared her throat, taking a pair of glasses out of a shiny black case and perching them on the end of her nose. "Thank you," she said. "My name is Alyssa Johnstone."

Kidd turned to Joe again. "Mr Warrington, is also present, would you mind stating your name for the tape?"

Joe cleared his throat and leant forward a little. "My name is Tony Warrington."

Kidd froze. "Excuse me?"

"Oh," Joe, or Tony, sat up straight. "Sorry, did you want my full name?"

Kidd's mouth hung open, catching flies.

Tony, or Joe, cleared his throat. "My name is Anthony Philip Warrington," he said, his voice actually shaking a little this time. "Is that okay?"

Kidd still stared dumbstruck. "Yes, fine, absolutely," Kidd said, sitting back in his chair. "You're not Joe."

"What?"

"You're not Joe Warrington," Kidd said, firmly.

Tony scoffed. "No, of course not," he said. "Joe's my twin. Younger by a whole ten minutes though. I'd show you my ID but they took it off me at the front desk. It's in my wallet. You can go and look if you like, I don't mind."

"I'm sorry," Alyssa chimed in. "What is going on here? Is my client not under arrest?"

"Sir, your phone is ringing," DC Campbell whispered next to him.

Kidd pulled his phone out of his pocket, seeing it was Zoe and flicked it to silent. He tried to think back to what she'd said about the Warringtons before, trying to remember.

She mentioned a brother, Kidd thought. *She never said he was a bloody identical twin. Shit.*

Kidd took a breath and sat forward in his chair. "It does appear that there has been some sort of mix up," Kidd said, feeling heat pricking his cheeks, not wanting to acknowledge quite how bad this looked for him, for the force. Weaver would have his head on a pike outside his office for this.

"Why didn't you wait for a positive ID? It's my head that's going to be in the smasher for this one! Are you out of your bleeding mind?" he would rage. Kidd could already feel the spittle peppering his face when he got the hairdryer treatment.

He'd rushed into it and he knew it.

"If my client isn't under arrest then I assume he is

free to go?" Alyssa's eyes were drilling into him with the intensity of a thousand suns. She wasn't impressed at being called out for no good reason at what was likely the end of her day.

"Yes, technically he is," Kidd said somewhat sheepishly. Tony moved to leave but Kidd held out a hand. "However, we would love to ask you a few questions about your brother, if that's okay?"

Alyssa sighed. "I can stay if you want me to," she said to Tony. "I'm charging your father either way."

Tony smiled at her sweetly. It was in that moment that Kidd saw the difference between the two brothers. While Joe had been surly and somewhat aggressive with him on the two occasions they'd met, here was Tony being kind.

"You can go if you like," Tony said. "I'm happy to talk to them about Joe."

Alyssa smiled, sighed, then stood up. "I'd love to say it's been a pleasure, but that wouldn't be true," she said with a smirk. "See you again."

"DC Campbell, would you mind showing Ms Johnstone out?"

"Absolutely," Campbell replied, jumping up and hurrying to the door to show her the way. This left Kidd alone with Warrington, something he definitely preferred because he didn't exactly want Campbell to see him apologising or admitting fault.

Kidd stopped the recording and leant back in his chair.

"I'm very sorry about all this, Tony," he said.

"It's not a bother." Tony shrugged, following suit and leaning back in his seat.

"Well, getting arrested and brought into a police station is hardly how anybody would want to spend their evening, I imagine," Kidd said, laughing a little, trying to ease the tension. "You both look so alike and, well, we're trying to bring your brother in for a pretty serious crime. I saw someone who looked like him, not knowing that he had a twin, and jumped at the chance to… well… to wrap this case up. I'm sure you understand."

Tony nodded. "Of course," he said. "But what do you want to know about Joe? How much trouble is he in?"

Kidd wasn't entirely sure how to approach this. The thing about having a sibling was that you wanted to protect them from things. Especially when they were younger, even if it was just ten minutes. If he was in a situation like this with Liz, what would he do? How would he react to being questioned? How much would he be willing to give away if he knew that it might end up getting her in trouble?

He couldn't be sure.

"We have reason to believe that Joe could be caught up in a murder case," DI Kidd said simply. "The victim was close to Joe, and we want to find him to… rule him out, if we can."

"But you're not going to be ruling him out, are you?" Tony replied. "You think he did it."

DI Kidd knew that was where the evidence was pointing at this point. Everything about what had happened so far told him that it was Joe Warrington, it was the only logical explanation. But then there was the feeling in his gut that told him otherwise. But he couldn't show that to Tony, he needed to appear certain.

"I think he might have, yes," DI Kidd said. "And that's why we're trying to find him as quickly as possible." He took a moment, knowing he was laying it on a little thick here, but hoping it would get through to Tony. "Before he has a chance to hurt anyone else."

Tony's face dropped. He'd spent so much time with his father talking badly about the police, maybe laying it on thick was what he needed to get through to him.

"I need you to tell me as much as you can about Joe," Kidd said. "I get the impression that you knew him better than anybody else, even your mum and dad, am I right?"

Tony nodded. "Yeah, I guess. Maybe it's a twin thing, I don't know," he said. "But we always had a weird connection that mum never really got. But she always told me to look out for him."

"And you telling us whatever you can, is doing just that," Kidd pressed. "Please, Tony, I wouldn't ask if I didn't have to. And you know it's the right thing, deep down, you must know that."

Tony took a breath and brought his eyes up to meet Kidd's. He really did look remarkably like Joe. If you put the two of them next to one another, there was no way that Kidd would have been able to tell them apart. They must've gotten up to an awful lot of mischief when they were younger, must've driven their poor mum mad.

"Joe is studying film and journalism," Tony said. "He's always liked cameras, just like me, and we always used to make little films together when we were at home. Nothing proper, like just stupid stuff, things we thought would get us famous on YouTube but mostly got us ignored and a little bit picked on at school." He laughed as he remembered something, the smallest glimmer in his eyes. He shook it from his head. "I used to film for him all the time," Tony added.

"For what?"

"For his social media stuff," Tony said. "I stopped wanting to be on the camera so much, enjoyed being behind it a lot more. He really got into documentary film making, what he called proper, hard-hitting stuff, and I started making more artsy films. We drifted in that way, I suppose, but I was always there to lend a hand if he needed my help with anything. It can be hard being a one-man band."

"So what changed?" Kidd asked.

"What's that?"

"You said you drifted," Kidd said. "How much did you drift? What pushed that rift between you, not just the film making?"

"No," Tony said, shaking his head. "The thing about Joe is that he was always a bit obsessive. He would grab onto something he really liked and just hammer it and hammer it and hammer it until he either hated it or he'd perfected it."

"So he was a difficult filmmaker to work with?"

"Impossible." Tony sighed. "He wanted everything

done a certain way, to the point where I eventually told him to just do it by himself. We got into a bit of a fight and…"

"And what, Tony?"

"Well, we've not spoken for a week," Tony said. "It's weird. We've never gone this long without speaking but…"

He trailed off and stared at the floor, sliding his shoe off and then back on again.

"What, Tony?"

"He started doing things on his own a couple of months back," Tony said, not to Kidd, just into space. He didn't seem to want to focus on Kidd at all at this point. Maybe he felt like he was betraying his brother in some way by talking to Kidd so candidly. "And I told him he was getting obsessed again and taking it too far, but then he started acting weird."

Kidd leaned in, his elbows on the table. "Weird how?"

CHAPTER
THIRTY-FOUR

Zoe scrambled to pick her phone up off the floor, quickly hanging it up, and shoving it into her pocket as she took in the sheer state of Colin's living room. With all the lights on, it looked like a war zone, like a bomb had hit it, hardly the clean and tidy home that she and Kidd had visited just twenty-four hours earlier.

Her focus was pulled to two parts of the room. Groggily, a figure in a dining chair on one side of the room lifted their head and looked across at Zoe. Her eyes widened, her hair matted with sweat, tears quickly springing to her eyes and running down her face.

On the other side of the room, sprawled out on the floor was Colin Hansen. Surrounding his head was a little blood, not much, mind, but enough to send an adrenaline surge through Zoe, enough to make her heart quicken, and know that she needed to take a few quick breaths and figure out what on earth she needed to do next. There was a dog next to him on the floor, not moving. Zoe didn't want to think about what had happened there.

This had not been what she'd expected.

"Deep breaths, Lydia, deep breaths," Zoe said as she hurried over to the girl in the chair. "Is the house empty?"

Lydia nodded, whimpering through the gag that was covering her mouth. Her skin looked pale, heavy bags under her eyes. She wondered just how long she'd been here, suddenly wishing she'd done more, that she'd tried harder to track her down.

"Good, good, good," Zoe said. "Deep breaths, okay? I need to check on Colin."

She hurried over to him and knelt at his side. She felt for a pulse. Thankfully able to feel one, the blood around his head coming from a small cut. Whoever had done this maybe hadn't been expecting him and clocked him around the head and then assumed he was dead. She needed to call an ambulance. She needed to call Kidd. She needed to untie Lydia.

One thing at a time, she thought.

She headed over to Lydia and untied her arms from behind the chair and her legs, slowly untying the gag from the back of her head. Lydia let out a heaving breath when it came free, bent double trying to get air into her lungs as quickly as possible. Zoe rubbed her back, reminding her she was here. She must have been scared out of her wits.

Zoe took her phone out of her pocket and called it in, giving them the address and telling them to come as soon as possible. By the time she had finished, Lydia was upright again, looking a few shades calmer.

"I thought… I didn't know… I thought I was…" She had hardly said more than a few words and it was like she could barely catch her breath. All Zoe wanted to do was hold her and tell her that it was all going to be alright, but she knew that they weren't out of the woods yet. She needed to know who had done this to her.

"Deep breaths, Lydia, deep breaths," Zoe said, bending down a little so she was at Lydia's level, trying to make eye contact with her to show her that at least one of them was calm. Maybe it would be enough to stop her having a panic attack. "There's an ambulance on the way for Colin. Everything's going to be alright."

"Is… is he…?"

"He's alive," Zoe said. "He's still breathing, got a nasty bump to the head. But don't worry about him right now, Lydia, okay? Let's focus on you. You need to tell me what happened."

She turned back to Zoe and looked like she was about to burst into tears on the spot. The tears filled her eyes and her breath was still coming in heaving gasps.

"What did I say about breathing?" Zoe said, giving her a quick nudge. Lydia did as she was told, taking a few breaths until she was able to look Zoe in the eyes again. "Now, tell me what happened, Lydia. Please."

"I was so scared," she said. "I thought he was going to kill me. I thought…" She stumbled over it, almost like she couldn't believe the words were about to come out of her mouth. And it came out in such a whisper. Zoe was only able to hear it because they were stood so close to one another. "I thought I was going to die."

CHAPTER
THIRTY-FIVE

"We just started spending less and less time together," Tony said. "Any time I did see him, he was snarky with me, like he didn't want anything to do with me. Like I was in his way or something. And he got really secretive about all the tapes that he had."

"Tapes?"

"Video footage," Tony said. "Got really precious about it, wouldn't let me see them. Mum was telling me to leave him be and let him do his work, even dad was being a bellend about it, but they don't know him like I do." Tony looked at DI Kidd now. "You said it yourself. They both knew we were closer than all that."

"Okay," DI Kidd said, leaning back in his chair. "Then what?"

"I stopped trying after a while, and that was when he disappeared, went off the grid," Tony said. "He messaged me about it, told me not to tell mum, and I didn't because…" Tony sighed and shook his head. "Because I'm an idiot. I didn't press him on it either, I just let him vanish off the face of the earth and now…" Tony trailed off and leant forward onto the table, putting his head in his hands. His shoulders shook a little, a couple of heavy breaths leaving him.

DI Kidd sighed. "Now, now, Tony, you can't go beating yourself up about this," he said. "Everything you're telling me is good. Keep going, keep going, yeah?"

"That's it," Tony said. 'That's all I've got for you, DI Kidd, I'm sorry." Tony looked up at Kidd, his eyes exactly the same. Kidd had expected to at least see a few tears but maybe that bastard dad had beaten that kind of behaviour out of them. But it still didn't sit right with Kidd. "If I could tell you any more I would."

"I'm sure," DI Kidd said, keeping his tone even, though now there really was something not sitting right with him. "But you mustn't beat yourself, Tony, you've done a good thing today telling us all that. And if you hear from Joe—"

"I'll give you a call," Tony said, cutting him off. "I won't hesitate. I know my dad can be a bit of a knob, but I know you're just trying to do the right thing. Even if it is to catch my little brother." Tony forced a smile onto his face and DI Kidd did the same.

There was a horrible feeling in DI Kidd's gut that he couldn't let go of. It was a feeling that he followed most of the time, but right now, he needed to let it go. He stood up, Tony quickly following suit.

He reached out a hand for Tony to shake, which he did gladly, giving a firm grip before he led the boy out of the room.

"Do you want me to arrange to have one of the officers drive you back home?" Kidd asked. "I know this is a little bit out of your way. I'm sure you want to get home."

Tony seemed a little caught off guard by that, looking off down the corridor and back at Kidd.

"No, don't worry about it," Tony said. "It's not that far and the bus goes from just out there," he nodded towards the door. "I'll be alright."

"You sure?" Kidd said. "It's not a bother. I'll get Campbell to do it. He's probably slacking in the Incident Room after he showed your lawyer out."

"It's fine," Tony said. "'I'll be alright."

"No, no," Kidd said. "I insist."

He didn't give Tony another chance to respond, heading in to collar DC Campbell whose hand was in a tub of Celebrations leftover from Christmas.

"Can you give the lad a lift home?" Kidd asked. "Think we owe him at least that much."

Campbell looked a little deflated, grabbing a Teaser and popping it into his mouth as he joined Kidd in the corridor.

They walked Tony to the door, buzzing him out into the reception area. He got his things off Diane and then walked out of the front door with Campbell, waving to Kidd on his way out, a big smile on his face. It was only as Kidd watched him walk away, that he noticed the way he walked, a slight limp, like he'd done something to his ankle. He wondered if he'd gotten hurt when they'd arrested him. He certainly didn't want that to come back and bite him.

"Letting him go, DI Kidd?" Diane said, leaning across the counter. "I don't know about you, but I thought you'd got your man."

Kidd looked off after Tony, watching him pull his jacket up around his ears and zip it up tight. The walk was strange. There was something Kidd couldn't quite put his finger on.

"Me too," he grumbled. "Me too. But I think we're getting closer."

Diane smiled at him courteously. "I should hope so. Dangerous out there."

He gave her a tight-lipped smile. "Agreed," he said, before heading back down the corridor and back towards the Incident Room, unable to shake the feeling that he'd done something wrong.

He stepped inside, returning to his desk and sitting behind it, going through the interview in his head again. Tony had seemed remarkably calm in the face of his brother being accused of murder. He tried to replay it, tried to read him, but decided the only thing left to do was track down Joe Warrington. They would need hard evidence, they would need to get his DNA and match it to whatever had been found on Jennifer Berry's body, and wrap it all up.

He remembered that Zoe had phoned him, taking his phone out of his pocket and seeing she had left a voicemail, he put it to his ear to listen to it when DC Ravel suddenly stood up.

"DI Kidd, you're going to want to take a look at this," she said. She looked jittery, nervous, excited. It was infectious. Kidd hung up the phone and got to his feet.

"You got something good?" he asked as he pocketed his phone once again.

"Confirmation, sir," DC Ravel said as Kidd walked around her desk to look over her shoulder at her computer screen. She opened the video file that had been sent over from Belmarsh prison, bringing it to full screen so that DI Kidd could see what she was so excited about.

And it was clear as day, right in front of his face.

"When is this from?" Kidd asked, trying to stop the shake in his voice. "When did it arrive?"

"While you were in the interview, sir," Ravel said. "It's from about two months ago, way before the Jennifer Berry murder."

"Does that line up with the timeline of his visits to Colin?"

DC Ravel leant around her computer to look at DC Powell. "Powell, did you get those dates for me?"

DC Powell scurried out from behind his desk, a couple of papers in his hands, and showed them to DC Ravel. She looked up at Kidd and smiled, triumphant. "They match up exactly," she said.

Kidd leant down and took hold of the mouse, rewinding the video again to watch as the image of Joe

Warrington walked into Belmarsh prison, shuffled sheepishly up to the desk, and spoke to the same woman that he'd spoken to just yesterday.

"That's him," Kidd said, but looked carefully at it once again. He rewound it and watched it one more time.

"Problem, sir?" DC Ravel asked.

He studied it again. "No," Kidd said. "Just checking to make sure. Now we just need to find him, right?" Kidd added, feeling that jitter in his stomach. He wanted to move quickly, *needed* to.

He felt his phone buzzing in his pocket and took it out, seeing it was another call from Zoe. If it was important enough for her to call again, she really must have had something important to say.

"Zoe, I'm sorry. I was in an interview with Tony Warrington, you'll never believe what happened," he said.

"Don't have time for that, Kidd, sorry," Zoe spat, her breath distorting down the receiver. "You need to get to Colin's house, and you need to get here *now.*"

CHAPTER
THIRTY-SIX

"I've got Lydia, she's fine but she'd been tied up. Colin is in a bad way," she said. "I just need you to get down here as soon as possible. I don't know how long the ambulance is going to be or if he's going to come back."

"Okay, try and keep Lydia calm. Can you get here out of the house?" he said making for the door.

"Why?"

He growled. "We've just let Tony go," he replied. "I need you to get her out of the house if you can, get her somewhere safe."

"Thanks, Kidd. Hurry," she added quickly.

"Gotcha," Kidd said down the phone. "Be there as quick as we can. Hang on, alright?"

Zoe ended the call and the house fell silent except for the sound of Lydia's heavy breathing next to her. Her hands were shaking, shaking so much it was a wonder she hadn't dropped her phone. Zoe pocketed her phone and turned back to Lydia, putting her hands on her shoulders, willing her to calm down, for her breathing to slow.

"You don't need me to tell you to calm down again," Zoe said. "I know it was scary, but the sooner you can tell me exactly what happened, the sooner we can get to the bottom of this, okay?"

Lydia took a breath and sat back down on the chair, putting her head in her hands. Zoe crouched in front of her. "It's just hard to believe," Lydia said. "I… I never thought that…"

"Never thought what, Lydia?" Zoe asked.

She looked up at Zoe, tears in her eyes. "I never thought that I would ever be so close to someone who would want to hurt me like that," Lydia said. "He grabbed me, he drugged me, he tied me up, I… Maybe it was instinct, I don't know, but I knew exactly what he was going to do with me. Like I should have realised the whole time that it was him."

Her hand flew to her mouth as she took a shuddering breath. "He was supposed to be my friend," she whispered. "Who would want to do something like that to their friend? And to do that to Jenny, too? He told me. He told me it was her, I didn't want to believe…"

Zoe placed a careful hand on Lydia's leg. She flinched. She really was in a bad way. Zoe kept her hand there and gave her a squeeze, hoping it would be somewhat reassuring to her, that it would help to calm her in some way.

"I hate to say it, Lydia," Zoe started. "And I don't

want this to colour your feelings about the world, but you never know what's going on in people's heads, never really know what they're capable of. More often than not, when someone is attacked or hurt, it's someone they know." Zoe sighed. "It might not be a comforting fact, but it is a true one."

"You just never think for a second that—"

There was a sound at the front door. Zoe stood up so quickly she gave herself a head rush. She steadied herself, placing a hand on the back of the chair before putting her body between Lydia and the door.

"Lydia?" a voice shouted. A voice that Zoe recognised. She tensed. She wasn't about to give away their position, wasn't about to—

"In here!" Lydia called back. Zoe looked at her sharply. She'd gotten up from the chair and was looking towards the doorframe hopefully, her eyes still a little glassy.

Zoe couldn't shake the confusion from her head as Joe Warrington stood in the door in front of her. Lydia moved to cross the room towards him but Zoe's arm shot out to stop her.

"What are you doing?" Lydia asked.

"I could ask you the same question," she replied before turning to look back at Joe. "Stay where you are!" she barked, her voice changing so drastically from one moment to the next, it made Lydia jump. "No one is going to get hurt, you just need to stay exactly where you are." She took a breath. "There are already police on the way, there is no point in running, Joe." She shook her head at him. "This is the end of the line for you."

"What are you talking about?" Lydia asked, a nervous quake in her voice.

Zoe looked over at her once again, trying to decipher if she was joking or not. Was she in on this with him? Had this been some kind of ruse to lure her here? But Lydia just looked… lost. And now Zoe felt lost too.

A car pulled up outside, stopping furiously, tyres screeching. It was enough to calm Zoe. It had to be Kidd. He'd been quicker than even she had thought possible. But time seemed to be stretching and bending since the moment she'd walked into this house. She would be happy for all of this to be over.

"That's DI Kidd's car out there, Joe," Zoe said firmly. "It's over."

"What?" Joe looked panicked, frantic. "I don't know… what's happening? Lydia, why did you call me here? Is this a setup?"

"No, no, it's not a setup."

Zoe looked sharply at Lydia. "You called him? Why did you do that when he's the one that…" Zoe trailed off. Realisation falling over her like a wave.

"It wasn't Joe who did it," Lydia said. "It was Tony."

And with those words, the front door to Colin Hansen's house burst open.

CHAPTER
THIRTY-SEVEN

DI Kidd hung up the phone and hurried to DCI Weaver's office, his heart pounding so hard in his chest he was shaking.

"What?" Weaver barked when Kidd burst through the door. "Updates?"

"I've fucked up, boss," Kidd blurted.

He explained what had happened to DCI Weaver, explained the video, explained everything and the two moved as quickly as they could. Weaver got a response team to head down to Hansen's property, Kidd immediately dialled Campbell's mobile.

"Come on, come on," Kidd said into the receiver. It went to voicemail and he cursed his own stupidity, his own rotten luck.

DI Kidd sent DC Powell off to find DC Campbell and grabbed DC Ravel. Kidd drove like a maniac to get to Colin's property before anything else could go wrong. His heart was pounding hard in his chest, threatening to break out from underneath his shirt. It all came down to this moment, of that much he was certain. And Zoe was in there.

When they pulled up outside the house, it was clear to see that they had beaten everybody else here. The door was hanging off the hinges, a car on the drive that Kidd immediately recognised as Campbell's. Without thinking, Kidd jumped out of the car and ran over to Campbell's vehicle, looking inside for his body, for any signs of damage, but finding nothing.

"Fucking hell," he growled.

"Anything, sir?" DC Ravel asked. He turned sharply to see her behind him, pulling her jacket around herself.

"Nothing," he said, turning his attention back to Colin's house. It was deathly quiet, which wasn't a good sign. That wasn't a good sign for anybody, least of all Zoe.

"Is DS Sanchez…?" Ravel started. "I offered to come with her sir, she told me not to."

"Don't go thinking this is your fault, Janya," Kidd said, trying to keep his voice even when it was violently shaking, The adrenaline was too much. *The only person whose fault this is, is mine*, he thought, looking up at the darkened house, a house that held so many horrors for DI Kidd.

I shouldn't have let her go on her own, he thought, scolding himself for even letting that happen. *Or I should've answered the bloody phone. Always answer your bloody phone, Kidd!*

"Boss?" DC Ravel called, looking down the street at

some blue lights off in the distance. "The cavalry's arrived."

"About bloody time," Kidd grumbled. DC Ravel turned to him and raised an eyebrow. "Tell them I've already gone in."

"No, you bloody won't." Weaver's voice stopped Kidd in his tracks. He'd parked a little way down the street, walking the rest of the way. His timing was bloody impeccable, as always. "You will wait out here until the armed officers arrive. Who knows what's going on in there."

"Exactly!" Kidd growled. "Zoe is in there."

"DS Sanchez is more than capable of handling herself."

"I'm not disputing that," Kidd said. "I'm disputing the fact that she is in there with a bloody murderer and I'm the one that let him walk free."

DCI Weaver blinked. He looked to the house and then back at Kidd. There wasn't really any arguing with that.

"I have to go in, boss. I have to fix it," Kidd said. "I've got two officers on my team in trouble and I need to fix it. I couldn't get through to Campbell. I'd already sent him off to drive Tony home. This is Campbell's car." He gestured to the haphazardly parked car on the drive.

"Where is DC Campbell?"

"That's a really good question, sir," DI Kidd replied. "We're trying to figure that out."

"What on earth has happened?"

"Campbell was driving Tony Warrington home,"

Kidd explained. "It's a bit of a guess at this stage, but I would say that Tony clocked Campbell over the head and tossed him from the car before driving it here and heading inside."

"Where—?"

"Where DS Sanchez is, with Lydia Jones and an unconscious Colin Hansen," Kidd interrupted. "I'm not asking you to go against protocol here, sir. I'm telling you that I am going inside right now because I need to finish this."

"DI Kidd, I can't let you—"

"I don't care, Weaver," Kidd interrupted again. "You might not want me to go in there, but I'm not about to leave DS Sanchez in there by herself. She is more than capable of handling herself, I know that first hand, but if she ends up hurt, I won't forgive myself. I can't go through that again."

DCI Weaver opened his mouth to respond. Kidd looked into his eyes, watching the cogs turning, the engine turning over but not quite managing to start. He didn't seem to have an argument, and it was all the permission that Kidd needed to go inside and finish the job.

He ignored the blue lights flying down the road behind him, pulling up outside the house. He could hear Weaver saying something to them, maybe giving him a time limit before they waded in, all guns blazing. He wanted to bring Tony in alive if he could. Just like Albert, he wanted him to suffer for what he'd done, for the pain he'd caused.

He stepped through the front door. He could see that somebody—Tony most likely—had kicked the thing in upon arriving. The only light inside was coming from the living room. The door was closed. He didn't want to imagine what was going on behind that door, didn't want to picture the chaos that awaited him. Nevertheless, he reached down and turned the handle, ready to face the beast within.

CHAPTER
THIRTY-EIGHT

"Don't move!" Tony's voice barked the second Kidd opened the door even the tiniest amount. "Who is it?" Kidd didn't know whether it was safer to answer or not. "WHO IS IT?"

"It's DI Kidd!" he replied, keeping his voice firm, strong. "Tony? That's you, isn't it?" He didn't reply. He could hear whimpering. He didn't know where it was coming from, whether the sound was male or female, but it didn't fill him with an awful lot of hope. "Tony, I think it is you," Kidd continued. "And I know that you're a sensible lad, alright? And because you're sensible, I'm going to come into the room. I promise you, I am on my own. There's no one with me."

"I said, don't move!" Tony barked, more strangled this time. The whimpering became more pronounced. "Don't come any closer."

"There's no one with me, Tony," Kidd said. "It's alright. I just want to talk to you."

"No, you don't."

"Yes, Tony, I do."

"You think I can't see the blue lights outside?" Tony said, a laugh managing to come through the mania. "You think I can't hear the voices? I know there are people out there. I know you've brought them here."

Kidd took a breath and tried again. "I'm on my own, Tony. You have my word on that, alright? I've not got anyone with me. I'm just going to come inside. There's no need to worry, no need to do anything drastic."

Tony started shouting again, the words coming out jumbled, muffled as two voices joined in with the shouts, one coming through a little stronger than the other. One he recognised as DS Sanchez.

Kidd stepped into the room and shut the door behind him, putting his hands in the air so Tony could see them. On one side of the room, he could see Zoe and Lydia as close to the window as possible, Zoe in front of Lydia, Lydia's face crumpled as she quietly cried. He couldn't blame her. Like it wasn't enough to have seen a dead body in the past week, she was probably supposed to be the next one. He wondered what had happened. Maybe she'd figured it out before they had. Maybe she'd gone digging around in Tony's business and it was enough to cause this.

Then there was Tony.

He was still wearing the same grey t-shirt and joggers he'd been wearing when they'd let him go. There were sweat stains on the pits of the tee. In front of him, the shiny blade of a knife was pressed to Joe Warrington's pale, white neck. That was a twist that Kidd hadn't been expecting.

"See?" Kidd said, finding his voice. "No one's with me, Tony. It's just me." He looked over at DS Sanchez. "You alright?"

She shrugged. "Been better," she said. "You took your time. Well done on letting the murderer go."

"Penny dropped a smidge too late," Kidd said. "I'm out of practice."

"Stop it!" Tony barked, pressing the knife a little harder to Joe's neck. His brother whimpered, tears in his eyes. "I told you not to come in."

"You're right, Tony, you told me not to come in," he said. "But you told me that you were worried about your brother. It looks to me like you're not all that worried about him after all."

"Shut up."

"I'd say we're even, Tony, yeah?" Kidd said. "I don't want to hurt you, alright? I don't want anything to happen to you, and I certainly don't want anything to happen to Joe." He shifted his gaze to Joe Warrington who locked eyes with him. Eyes that pleaded with him, eyes just like his mother's. He turned his gaze back to Tony. "So let's talk."

"I'm sick of talking," Tony said. "We did enough talking."

"Yeah, and you thought you'd got me, didn't you?" Kidd said. "You almost did."

"I know I did. You coppers are all the same, thick as

shit," Tony spat. "I was in your bloody station, right in your hands and you couldn't even get it right."

"Five minutes either way, Tony, and I wouldn't have let you out of that station. I'd have slammed you in a cell and you'd be going down for murder."

"I didn't!" he shouted.

Kidd couldn't believe what he was hearing. "What the bloody hell do you mean, you didn't?" Kidd shouted. "You killed her, Tony. You killed Jennifer Berry, you left the body in Bushy Park, you sliced her open. How can you say you didn't—?"

"I didn't mean to!" he shouted over him. And it was in that moment that Kidd could see the fear in the young boy's eyes. Absolute terror. "It was an accident."

Kidd did his utmost not to scoff in the boy's face. He did have a knife to his brother's throat, after all. He didn't want to antagonise him. But an accident? Even the suggestion of that made Kidd feel sick to his stomach. How could he say it was an accident after everything he did to her?

"Explain yourself," Kidd demanded. "I don't see how it could have been an accident, Tony, the way she was left—"

"I had to do something," he snapped, tightening his grip on Joe, who somehow managed to look even more panicked than he had done just a moment before. Kidd needed to tread carefully here, keep him talking if he could. "She… I cared for her," Tony said eventually. "We were making a film. We'd been making it for a long time. So long, that I'd grown attached to her in a way."

He stared off past Kidd, wistfully, like he was seeing her in his mind's eye, the very mention of her taking him back to a moment when he wasn't in a place such as this.

"Go on," Kidd said.

"She was my muse," he said looking at Kidd. "We worked so well together. It was beautiful, really. And I wanted more than that. So, I tried to offer her more and she said no. I didn't want to jeopardise the film we were making, she really was wonderful in it, a terrific actress."

And you took that away from her, Kidd thought.

"And so when we were filming in the park, I tried again, and she got upset with me. Very upset with me, in fact, and she started to fight with me about it. She got angry, physical, pushing me. I pushed her back. I didn't mean to push her so hard, but I was frustrated and… and she fell."

"She fell?"

"She hit her head on a rock jutting out from the ground," Tony said, looking down at the floor like he could see it, like he could see her lying there. "I said her name over and over again but she didn't respond. She was just quiet on the ground. Bleeding."

"But why The Grinning Murders, Tony?" Kidd asked. "Why go to those lengths? Why do all of that to her?"

"To hide it," Tony said. "I'd seen what Albert Hansen had done. He was going to be my next project. I'd been talking to Colin for weeks at that point. I'd been to see him in prison, I'd seen how he'd done it. I thought… I thought if I did it… if I copied him then no one would ever think… that no one would ever find out…"

He looked over at Lydia, his mouth turning into a snarl. "But someone knew a little bit too much, didn't they?"

Lydia cowered away, getting closer and closer to the window. Tony's hand was shaking.

"You just couldn't keep it to yourself, could you? You had to try and go all Nancy Drew, didn't you, Lydia? Couldn't leave well enough alone!"

"She was my friend!" Lydia shouted.

"She was more than a friend to me!" Tony shouted back.

"And what about Joe?" Kidd said, bringing his attention off Lydia. It wouldn't do well to get him all worked up. "Why would you try to frame Joe?"

He looked down at his younger brother, someone he was supposed to protect, to look out for.

"He's always thought he was better than me," Tony snarled. "No matter what I did, it was never good enough for mum and dad. We go to the same university, who are they proud of? Little Joseph for moving out. Joseph's got the social media following. Joseph's making a career for himself, what are *you* doing, Tony? Huh? Joseph, Joseph, Joseph!"

"But framing your own brother," Kidd said, "that's pretty low."

"Then maybe I am low!" Tony barked. "Maybe I am. But I had you fooled, didn't I?" The knife moved steadily away from Joe's neck. His grip around his brother loosening as he focussed entirely on Kidd. "I had you for a while, didn't I? Had everybody thinking it was little Joe. So close."

Kidd shook his head. "You think you're as clever as Albert Hansen? You're nothing but a cheap imitation."

Kidd practically watched the words float across the space between them and smack Tony in the face. The anger etched into his every expression deepened, became more pronounced, and Kidd knew this would be his only chance.

Kidd burst forward. His brother distracted, his grip not quite as tight, Joe knocked Tony out of the way. It was enough to make Tony stumble, enough for him to swing wildly with the blade in a panic.

Kidd dodged, raising his arm and earning himself a brand new cut to go along with the bruise Joe had given him the day before. He really wasn't having much luck with the Warringtons.

"He's going for the door, Kidd!" Zoe barked.

Kidd bolted for the living room door, watching as Tony flew through it, and out into the night. Into the waiting arms of the police. But Kidd knew better than that. He had a knife. Either they would shoot him or he would hurt himself before they could. He'd seen it happen one too many times, read one too many police reports, and he wasn't about to let that happen this time.

He flew out after Tony, who had stupidly stopped in the glare of the headlights. Kidd took his chance and dove at him, knocking the blade from his hand and the wind out of him as he hit the cold, hard concrete.

CHAPTER
THIRTY-NINE

The ambulance arrived and tended to Colin Hansen, checked that the dog was alright, too. Turned out, Tony had kicked the absolute living daylights out of him to stop him yapping, but he would be alright. While that was going on, Kidd stole a quiet moment to get his arm looked at and get it dressed. It had bled pretty heavily onto his white shirt, which was only good for the dustbin now. That was one bloodstain that wouldn't come out anytime soon, not that he wanted to try. He wouldn't want to be reminded of everything that had happened tonight, anyway, if he could help it.

"That was some piece of detective work you did there, DI Kidd." Weaver appeared in front of him as he sat on the back of the ambulance, having his arm wrapped up in a bandage by the young, male paramedic. "How did you get to it?"

"I didn't look carefully enough," Kidd said. "I

would've gotten there quicker if I'd read the signs a little better. I got blinkered, really."

Weaver shrugged. "It happens to the best of us. At least no one was hurt."

Kidd raised an eyebrow at him.

"No one *else*," Weaver corrected. "Apart from yourself."

"I've had worse," Kidd replied. "It was the CCTV from the prison."

"What?"

He turned to the paramedic who was trying to keep his focus firmly on Kidd's arm. "Don't you listen to any of this," Kidd said. The young lad looked up and smirked at Kidd, who winked, making him look back down.

Weaver rolled his eyes so hard that Kidd could practically hear them.

"Tony had been to visit Hansen in prison a few times," Kidd said. When he'd got DC Ravel to replay the tape over and over again, he'd noticed the limp that Tony'd had. Joe didn't have that. He hadn't had it the whole time Kidd had seen him. It was the smallest thing, but it was enough to differentiate between the two of them. If he'd have seen the CCTV a few minutes earlier… who knows?

"He mentioned a documentary he was wanting to make," Kidd continued. "He said he'd been talking to Colin for that. But he kept on using Joe's name. Something tells me that, as much as he says killing Jennifer was an accident, there was an element of premeditation in there. The knife wounds, for one. You don't just make those if you've not been thinking about it. All the visits to Colin and Albert."

"You think Albert convinced him to do it?"

Kidd took a breath. The thought had crossed his mind when Tony had been telling his story. Kidd had seen firsthand just how persuasive, how snakelike Albert could be. But could he really talk someone into doing his dirty work for him? Was it a coincidence that Jennifer was the daughter of one of the previous victims? Kidd didn't know. He didn't like to believe that Albert Hansen had that power. He didn't want to believe that anybody did.

"I hope not, sir," Kidd said eventually. "I think he just got caught up in it. I'm not making excuses for him, not at all, but… I just hope not."

"Well, you did very well, Kidd," Weaver said, shoving his hands in his pockets. "I think I did the right thing bringing you back early, don't you?"

It was the closest thing DI Kidd would get to a compliment from Weaver, so he'd take it.

"I think I got lucky."

Weaver shrugged. "I think luck plays a bigger part in policing than any of us would like to admit," he said. "There's skill, there's detective work, there's being damn good at your job, but sometimes you just need the pieces to fall in your lap at the right time. Timing is everything."

"I've heard that," Kidd said.

"Get some rest, Kidd," Weaver said. "Take a couple of days off. I'll see you next week."

"See you next week, sir," Kidd said as Weaver walked back to his car. The police were still buzzing around Colin's house, picking up any evidence that they could, sweeping the whole place to make sure they could get an ironclad case against Tony. Despite the fact he'd admitted everything to Kidd, even in front of witnesses, it wasn't enough to convict. They'd need that confession on tape, and every bit of evidence they could find. They had his DNA now. It would only be a matter of time before they picked it up on Jennifer Berry. Then it would be curtains for Tony Warrington. At least, Kidd hoped it would.

The paramedic finished bandaging Kidd's arm and sent him on his way. He walked through the sea of flashing blue lights, along the cordon created by a thin piece of police tape. He looked up to see a few people down the street trying to see if there was anything worth gossiping about. It was just like old times.

"Admiring the scenery?" Zoe asked as she walked over to him. She'd left Joe and Lydia wrapped in blankets talking to a couple of uniformed officers.

"Something like that," Kidd said. "They okay?"

"They'll be alright," Zoe said. "They're a little bit shaken, which I think is fair enough given the circumstances, don't you?"

"I'll say."

"But they'll be fine."

"Shit!" Kidd said, reaching into his pocket and pulling out his phone.

"What?" Zoe asked. "You forget something? Got another murderer on the loose already?"

"No, I forgot about bloody DC Campbell, that's his car, something—"

"DC Powell's got it sorted, sir," DC Ravel said appearing at his side. "Got a call on the way in. Campbell got battered in the head by Tony's shoe, dragged out of the car, and left on the side of the road. He'd almost made it all the way here before DC Powell picked him up and took him to Kingston Hospital to get checked out."

"But he's okay?"

DC Ravel chuckled. "It's Campbell, so he's making a meal of it, but he's fine."

Kidd cleared his throat. "Thank you, Janya. That will be all for tonight, I think. Weaver's told me to go home, so I think it's about time you clocked off as well. Good job on this. Couldn't have done it without you."

DC Ravel smiled. "I know, sir. Thank you, sir," she said, nodding and walking away.

"I like her," Zoe said quietly.

"I thought you might," Kidd replied.

"And look at you getting all worried about DC Campbell," Zoe said. "If I tell him, you know he'll never let you live it down."

"If you tell him I'll…" he trailed off. Zoe laughed.

"You'll what?" she asked.

"I don't know, Zoe, I'm shattered. Can we just get to the part where you won't tell him?"

She laughed harder. "You're going to have to try a little harder than that. You're *definitely* out of practice!"

She laughed and hurried to catch up with Janya, saying something to her quietly before they both headed over to her car. She must have offered her a lift back to the office. Kidd checked his phone. It wasn't even all that late, nor had it even been that long since he'd started working on this case, but he could feel it had aged him. He could feel it in his bones.

He looked back at Colin Hansen's house, at Colin being put into the back of an ambulance. With all due respect to Colin, if he ever saw him again, it would be a day too soon. But he still had one more thing to say to Albert.

CHAPTER
FORTY

Kidd's body ached when he woke up the following morning. It had taken every bit of willpower that he had to drag himself out of bed and into the shower. His shoulders ached where he'd tackled Tony to the ground, his arm still stung from where Tony had caught him with that knife. But there was that sense of a job done. To say that it was *well* done, though, certainly felt like he was pushing it a little.

He got himself dressed in a pair of jeans and a t-shirt, grabbing his jacket from behind the door, before getting into his car and setting off. It wasn't all that early so the roads were a little bit of a nightmare, but he put a talk radio station on and allowed their words to wash over him as he drove. He didn't pay too much attention to it, just focussed on his destination.

When he pulled into the car park at HM Prison Belmarsh, he almost didn't get out of the car. He stared up at the building, dread twisting his stomach. He knew what was waiting for him in there, and he knew that he didn't have to do this. There was just something in him that couldn't let it go.

"This will be it," he told himself. "One last time and then it's buried, then it's gone. I won't have to think about it again."

Even Kidd didn't know whether that statement was true or not. You never forget your first. And The Grinning Murders had been Kidd's first, after all. It would probably haunt him to his grave. But he needed to at least try and find some closure if he could.

He headed inside as he had done before, the same receptionist looking glumly at her computer screen as he walked in, hardly even acknowledging his presence. He cleared his throat as he reached the front desk, her entire face brightening when she realised who it was.

"Good morning, Detective," she chirped. "How are we today?"

"Very well, thank you," he replied. "I just wanted to thank you for the information you sent over to us yesterday," he added quickly. "We wouldn't have tracked the guy down if it wasn't for you."

She smiled a little, apparently pleased to have helped. It was a stark contrast to the woman who'd wanted him out of her sight as quickly as possible just a couple of days ago.

It would be Weaver who'd likely get the credit for the investigation. Depending on what mood he was in, he may pass down some of the recognition to Kidd, who would then, in turn, pass it down to the rest of his team.

It was the right thing to do, after all. He knew a lot of officers who would take full credit, even if they'd been holed up in their offices the entire time, not daring to show their faces. Kidd would never be like that. He refused.

"It's alright" she replied. "I'm glad to hear it went well." A brief silence fell between them and she seemed to take him in a little more, perhaps noticing the clothes. "You didn't come all this way just to tell me that, did you?" she asked. "You certainly don't look dressed for work, DI Kidd, if you don't mind me saying."

Kidd chuckled. "I am here for work… somewhat."

She raised an eyebrow. "Somewhat?"

Kidd flashed her a smile. "I'd like to see Albert Hansen, please."

She eyed him carefully for a moment, trying to read him over the top of her spectacles, but just as she had done when he'd been here previously, she sighed heavily and grabbed the sign-in book for him and told him to wait to be taken through. It took a little longer this time than it had before but, just like last time, a prison officer arrived to take him through to see Albert Hansen.

The visiting room was much the same as it was before. There were a few more people in it this time, a couple of groups of people sitting across the table from people in their prison uniforms. Albert Hansen was on the far side of the room, watching the door with such intense curiosity, that Kidd had the opportunity to see his calm demeanour shift momentarily as he walked in the room. Perhaps he'd been expecting someone else. Kidd felt a grim satisfaction in that.

"Well, well, well," Albert said as Kidd sat down, trying to ignore the uncomfortable chair once again. "To what do I owe the pleasure?" He eyed Kidd carefully as he stared him down. "Take off your jacket, DI Kidd, you're making the place look untidy."

"No need," Kidd replied. "I shan't be staying long."

Albert narrowed his eyes at Kidd. "You're not coming down here to accuse me of puppeteering again, are you? It was boring last time, you coming down here with no evidence, accusing me of—"

"There's evidence this time, Hansen, so you might want to keep quiet for a change."

Hansen flinched, the words hitting him. Kidd could see him processing his way through them, trying to drill down to what Kidd had just said.

"What do you mean?" he asked eventually. The coolness had slipped. Kidd knew that he had him on the ropes and he wasn't about to give in now.

"You held out on me last time I was here," Kidd said, leaning back in his chair, feeling the plastic bow a little. "I asked you if you knew anything and you told me that you didn't. You tried to make me feel like I was completely out of my mind coming here to ask you questions about what was going on. But it turns out I was right all along." Hansen was unmoved. "Even after all these years, it seems my instincts about you are right. I knew it was you back then, I knew it was you now."

Hansen locked eyes with Kidd, the two of them

staring at one another from across the table. Kidd could see one of the prison officers watching them both intently. Perhaps Kidd's voice had been a little louder than he'd intended, but what he was seeing now was a standoff as Hansen tried to figure out his next move.

He laughed. "Well, you are a clever one, aren't you?" Hansen said. "Did you come all this way just to pat yourself on the back?"

"So you admit it?"

"I don't know what you're talking about, of course," Hansen said. "But I look forward to a case being made against me in court and not just you coming down here to toss yourself off in front of me."

"We caught Tony," Kidd said, and he could swear Hansen paled just a fraction. "You were a good teacher, he almost had us. You definitely taught him a thing or two about being a slippery bastard. Or was he a natural and that's why you chose him?" When Hansen didn't say anything, Kidd added, "Now, we're getting into nature versus nurture—whether murderers are born that way or if they're made—and I'm not about to have that conversation with you."

"I have my opinions about that."

Kidd smirked. "I'm sure you do. I don't want to hear them," he said. "Tony tried to run. Maybe that was another thing you taught him. He tried to run and I caught him, just like I caught you."

"Well, we do love a cinematic parallel, don't we?" Hansen said with a smile. "So, what did you come here for? If you're expecting remorse, you're not going to get any from me. I would have thought you'd know that by now."

Kidd laughed. He did know that. He'd known Hansen long enough to know that for certain. Kidd took a breath and leant forward, lowering his voice so that only Hansen would be able to hear.

"I'm not here to be congratulated. I'm not here to gloat," he hissed. "I'm not even here to get an apology from you or to make you feel bad. I'm here for closure. I'm here to tell you that it's over."

And without another word, Kidd stood up and started for the door, a prison officer quickly following behind him to guide him back.

"That's where you're wrong, Kidd!" Hansen shouted behind him. "It's never over! It is *never over!*"

Kidd didn't look back, refused to give him the satisfaction of any more of his attention. He let the prison officer close the door behind him, Hansen's words still ringing in his ears.

It's never over.

Kidd knew that, of course. There would be somebody different next week, or the week after. A different body, a different case, a different set of complications and a web he would need to navigate his way through if he was going to bring the guilty to justice. But at least next time, it wouldn't be Hansen. That, for now at least, had been laid to rest.

CHAPTER
FORTY-ONE

K idd returned home and spent the rest of the day relaxing. He didn't do anything strenuous. He didn't run. He didn't check his emails. He did his best not to flinch when he heard a police car or an ambulance whizzing by the house. He kept himself to himself the entire day, until his phone buzzed towards the end of the afternoon.

Drink?

It's Zoe, btw. In case you deleted my number :P

Kidd rolled his eyes and replied.

Sounds good to me. When? Where?

Druids. 6ish?

Perfect.

He got himself ready, throwing on a shirt and spritzing himself with a little bit of cologne for the first time in goodness knew how long. He wasn't about to go wild, he did have a job to go back to on Monday morning and the hangovers seemed to sting a little more as the years went by. He would take it easy, enjoy a nice night out with a friend. That would be enough.

————

Zoe had bagged a table by the time he got there. It was tucked away at the back of the downstairs area. While much of the pub was bathed in an orange sort of light, towards the back, they were cloaked in the shadows cast by the lamps, able to hide a little and people watch should they wish to.

Kidd grabbed the first round, taking his first sip of cider and sinking into his chair, letting out a breath he'd probably been holding all day.

"Christ, you look like you needed that," Zoe said, taking a sip of her own pint. "Maybe yours is different to mine, I'm not about to sink into my chair and have an orgasm over it."

Kidd choked. "Zoe, Christ!"

"What? You're choking at me saying orgasm?! Who died and made you head of the Catholic Church?" She chuckled and took another sip. "Oh, actually that's more like it, I see what you mean. Maybe the second sip is better."

Kidd shook his head at her and looked out over the throng of people crowded around the bar, their Saturday night just getting started.

"How are you feeling?" she asked.

"Oh Christ, you didn't bring me out for a heart to heart, did you?" he asked.

"No, Ben, nothing like that," she said. "I just wanted to know how you're doing. First big case under your belt since coming back. It's got to feel good, right?"

Kidd shrugged. "Something like that, yeah," he said, taking another sip. "I wish I'd gotten there faster."

"Kidd, you couldn't have done it any faster if you'd tried," Zoe said with a snort.

Kidd shook his head. "If we'd had the CCTV footage quicker, maybe we could've put two and two together a little bit faster and you wouldn't have ended up in that house."

Zoe shrugged. "If I hadn't gone there, you wouldn't have known where to go and then…" she trailed off. "It doesn't bear thinking about what might have happened."

Kidd knew he should just accept the win and move on, but there was something about not seeing things straight away, Tony managing to pull the wool over his eyes that made him question if he was in the right head-space to be doing this.

Zoe reached across the table and put a hand on his arm. He turned his gaze to her.

"Don't do that," she said. "I can see what you're doing."

"What?"

"You're spiralling," she said. "Now is not the time for spiralling, now is the time for toasting." She lifted her glass and reached across to him. Kidd followed suit and they clinked their glasses together, a satisfying dull clink. "You did a good job, we all did. And that needs to be celebrated before the next thing comes along."

"Can't wait," Kidd said with a wink.

"In the meantime," Zoe said, "we need to find you a hobby."

"Why does everybody want to find me a hobby?" Kidd groaned. "I run, I read, I watch TV, my life is full enough."

"It would be fuller with someone else in it, don't you think?" she replied, waggling her eyebrows. "What about the guy with the card?"

"What guy with the card?"

"Don't repeat what I'm saying to fill time," Zoe snarked. "You should call him."

She stared Kidd down, he stared back at her. "What, now?"

Zoe shrugged. "Why not? Life's short."

Kidd reached into his jacket pocket where John's card

was currently taking up residence. Zoe shook her head at him, but he didn't even want to entertain that. He dialled the number and nervously pressed the phone to his ear, trying to ignore the pounding in his chest.

John answered the phone pretty quickly. It was loud on his end. "Hello?"

"Hey," Kidd said down the phone. "Sorry, it's Ben from the bar the other night, is this a bad time?"

"No, not at all," he said in a hurry. "I didn't know if I was going to hear from you."

"Where are you? It's so loud."

John laughed. "Don't think less of me, but I'm actually at the pub again," he said.

Kidd froze.

"Hello? You still there?"

"Yeah, yeah, I am," he said. "I'm here too, actually."

It was John's turn to go silent. "You are? Where?"

"Uh," Kidd looked over at Zoe who was grinning so broadly she looked as if her face was about to split in two. "Near the back, right by the alcoves."

"Alright," John said. "I'll come and find you, hang on."

He hung up and Kidd returned his phone and the card to the pocket of his jeans.

"What's happening?" Zoe asked. "Did you lose reception or something?"

"No," Kidd said. "He's here. He's coming to find us."

Zoe's eyes widened. "Christ, Ben, I'm sorry," she said. "I know I was being super pushy but—"

"So, you've got a different woman on your arm

tonight?" John appeared near the table, a gin and tonic in his hand, a smile plastered across his face. "Am I getting the wrong idea here?"

"Not at all," Kidd said. "This is Zoe, a work colleague. Zoe, this is John."

Zoe waved. "A pleasure."

John turned his attention back to Kidd who was still sitting. It made him feel awkward, having John pretty much towering over him. It was more than a little unnerving.

"So, this isn't the best time to have a drink together, huh?" he said.

Kidd looked across at Zoe and then back to John. "Not really," he said. "Another time, though?"

John widened his eyes and nodded, taking a sip of his drink, possibly preparing his next move. "That works for me," he said. "I've got your number now."

"You sure do," Kidd said.

"So, I'll call you tomorrow," he said. "It was lovely meeting you, Zoe."

"And you."

"Bye," Kidd said as John walked away. He couldn't keep the smile off his face.

"Well, look at you beaming," Zoe said. "Looks like we might have found you a hobby."

Kidd practically choked on his drink. "You're terrible."

"And you can't do without me," she said, raising her glass to him before bringing it to her lips, unable to keep the smile off her face.

Kidd watched John walk away, the possibility of something new on the horizon. He was getting back on his feet and maybe things were going to be okay this time. Maybe.

DI BENJAMIN KIDD WILL RETURN IN

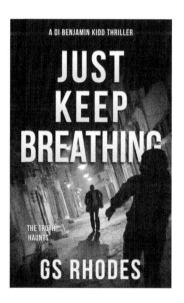

JUST KEEP BREATHING

Buy Now, or read on for the first three chapters…

JUST KEEP BREATHING

The truth haunts…

When Sarah Harper, a young girl from a rich family with a seemingly perfect life vanishes without a trace, there is an outpouring of grief from the community and all eyes are on DI Kidd and his team to get her found and get her found fast.

But nobody's life is as it seems. DI Kidd knows that more than most, and it isn't long before secrets start surfacing about Sarah and her family, cracking the veneer of their seemingly ideal existence. Suddenly everyone is a suspect and time is running out to bring the girl back alive.

With his boss breathing down his neck and the eyes of the world on him, Kidd is having to juggle his personal and professional life once again, a tightrope walk he has fallen from once and cannot afford to do again...

CHAPTER
ONE

S arah Harper's voice was hoarse from all the yelling, all the screaming. That's all her life seemed to have been for the past couple of days, a series of arguments with people that she thought were supposed to be on her side. All because of some stupid bloody pictures.

Well. A lot of stupid bloody pictures, come to think of it.

They'd all bought it though. They'd seen them fighting, seen them yelling at one another and crowded around like she'd expected them to. Some were filming it on their phones, others were taking pictures, they were all talking about her.

It was the only way to deal with it.

Her phone buzzed in her pocket. She took it out and couldn't help but smile at the message, before pocketing her phone and carrying on her walk.

She was avoiding going home. She knew that once she got there, her mum would be all over her wanting to know if she was okay, maybe even wanting to get some shots in for her own Instagram account. There were days when Sarah wondered if her life was a fashion accessory to her mother's "brand."

She shuddered.

The fact that her mother had a brand.

She walked through Kingston town with her hands in her pockets, her jacket, the one Dexter let her borrow at the start of their relationship, wrapped tightly around her, her legs exposed to the elements in her school uniform, not knowing where exactly to turn. If only all those people who'd enjoyed watching her downfall at school could see her now, it would certainly give them something to laugh about. To laugh at.

Sarah Harper with the perfect life.

Sarah Harper with the perfect boyfriend.

Sarah Harper with the perfect grades.

Perfect everything.

They had no idea. Not really.

She caught her reflection in the front of the Bentall Centre, her blonde hair being blown about by the wind, her cheeks a little flushed from the cold. To an outside eye, her perfect life was in tatters around her and she had no one else to turn to. And that was true to an extent. There were maybe two people she could call at a time like this. But she knew she shouldn't.

Sarah took out her phone and took shelter beneath the awning outside the front of the shopping centre. The stark white lights from inside leaked out and made her squint a little.

She rounded her shoulders, not wanting to be seen. It was so unlike her. She started scrolling through her friends, former friends, not finding a single name she could click on, a single person she could message. They'd all turned on her, every last one and—

"Sarah?"

The voice pulled her focus to a face that she recognised, maybe from a past life. She couldn't remember the last time she'd heard that voice.

"Hi," she said.

"What are you doing out here? You must be freezing."

She swallowed. "I am," she said. "Just got nowhere left to go, do I?'

A raise of an eyebrow. The shake of a head. "We both know that's not true."

And they walked. They walked blissfully unaware, into the beginning of a nightmare.

CHAPTER
TWO

For the past hour or so, DI Benjamin Kidd had not been a detective for the London Metropolitan Police, he hadn't been in charge of a team of four people tasked with bringing criminals to justice. The only things he'd been in charge of for the past hour were his niece and nephew. He was the storyteller, the climbing frame, the punching bag, you name it, he was it and he didn't mind at all.

"Alright, alright, it's bedtime!"

This elicited a groan from Tilly, the eldest, and just a series of babbles from Tim who didn't really know what was going on. But for Tilly, it was the voice of doom. Ben's sister, Liz, trudged into the living room, a tea towel slung over her shoulder. She looked at Kidd who was holding Tim, his six-month-old nephew, and three-year-old Tilly was hanging off his arm. "Thanks for watching them."

"Thanks for cooking dinner," Kidd replied with a

smirk. They were one of the shining points of his life. He loved coming around to see them and spending time with Liz. The kids loved him and he loved them. The best part being, when the night was over, he got to go home to a quiet house and not be disturbed by them at all hours of the night.

Between them, they put Tim and Tilly to bed, returning downstairs to find the house smelling so wonderful, Kidd's stomach growled involuntarily.

"Oh, sorry about that," he said. "Been a long day."

"You're not skipping meals are you?" Liz asked as she walked back to the kitchen.

"No, *Mum*, I'm not skipping meals," Kidd said. "Just been a busy time at work and when it's busy, I don't get the chance to breathe, let alone eat."

"Big case?" she asked.

"Not yet," he replied. There had been a lot of paperwork after the last case and he had a feeling that something else was around the corner. The scumbags of the world didn't like to give them a break if they could help it. Kidd had barely been back at work a month after being signed off with stress, and the case they'd brought him back to work, should have been enough to have him signed off all over again.

The Grinning Murders were a series of murders that had occurred fifteen years ago, when Kidd had first stopped being a uniformed officer and become a DC. When a body like that had shown up on the borough again, Detective Chief Inspector Patrick Weaver had wasted no time bringing him back. The copycat had been nothing more than a poor imitation, but it was still enough to give Kidd and his team the runaround.

They'd gotten news of the conviction today, a life sentence for what Tony Warrington did to Jennifer Berry. It was the outcome that they'd hoped for but didn't dare expect. It wasn't every day that you got a good result like that, so they basked in the win, allowing themselves to relax for the afternoon. But it would only be a matter of time before something else came along, sending them all over town trying to track down some nutcase who was running riot. Whatever it was, he hoped it didn't come too soon.

"Anything juicy?" Liz asked, opening the oven to check on the roast. The smell that wafted out almost had Kidd clutching his stomach. It certainly had his mouth watering.

"You're killing me here, Liz," he said with a smile. "It smells great."

She turned to him and raised an eyebrow. "I take that to mean you're not telling me a damn thing."

Kidd sighed. "I'm trying to get better at not talking about work all the time," he said. "I got obsessed. I need to be less like that, for my own sanity."

"Plus, you have someone else to occupy your time now," she said, a knowing look in her eye. "Do I get to meet him properly anytime soon or do I just have to suffer you making goo-goo eyes at your phone whenever he messages you?"

She was talking about John. John McAdams. Kidd had met him at a bar about two weeks ago, and deciding that maybe he didn't want to be alone for the rest of his life, had tentatively dipped his toe into the dating pool. He was still getting over the disappearance of Craig Peyton nearly two years ago, so it was baby steps, but things were looking up.

"You'll meet him at some point," Kidd said, heading to the fridge. "You want a drink?"

"You really are dodging everything I throw at you tonight, aren't you?" Liz said with a laugh. "I'm zero for two."

"Try harder," Kidd said, pulling a bottle of wine and a bottle of cider out. He moved to the cupboard to get glasses.

"So, your school reunion is this week, isn't it?"

Kidd made an involuntary shudder. "It is. I'm…I'm thinking of skipping it."

Liz mock gasped, her hand flying to her chest. "No, you missing a social event, it couldn't possibly be true!" She rolled her eyes and walked over to the cupboard where the glasses were, pulling out three wine glasses and a pint glass for his cider. "You should go."

"Do I have to?"

"No," she said. "But you never go out."

"I go out," he protested. "Why do we keep having this conversation?"

"Because you don't go out," she retorted. "You go out with John, you sometimes go out with your team, but this is meant to be fun. You can go there and you can flaunt your DI status to all the people who bullied you at school."

"And they can ask me for free legal advice?" he offered. "Or they won't tell me anything because they'll think I'm going to cuff them there and then."

"Kinky."

"LIZ!"

"I'm kidding," she groaned. "Stop being so dry all the time."

She lifted the lid off the veggies that were bubbling away on the stove, giving them a quick stab with a knife to check if they were done. She opened her mouth to speak again, probably to start another onslaught of harassment about him going out, when the doorbell rang.

"Saved by the bell," he said with a waggle of his eyebrows. "I'll get it."

He headed out of the kitchen and down the hall, opening the door to see DS Zoe Sanchez on the porch looking like a walking icicle. The breeze that came in with her drove its way right down into Kidd's bones. It really was fresh tonight.

She looked up at him and smiled. She'd let down her brown curls that she usually kept away from her face during the workday and had changed from her work get up into a pair of jeans and a sheer, black blouse. She'd even put on a little bit of makeup for the occasion.

"You look nice," Kidd said with a smile.

DS Sanchez's brow furrowed. "Implying that I don't usually?" she asked.

"Ha ha." Kidd rolled his eyes. "Come on in, I'm sorting drinks. Wine or cider?"

"Cider for me," she said, shrugging off her jacket and hanging it on the hooks by the door. "Sorry it took so long to get here. Got caught talking to Owen on my way out."

"Christ, poor thing," Kidd replied.

"He started talking about the case, the conviction and such, and then about going for a drink." Zoe walked into the kitchen. Her face brightened when she saw Liz. "Liz, you're looking well. It's been ages."

"Way too long!" Liz replied, hurrying over to wrap Zoe in a hug. She pulled out of the hug. "Okay, don't mind me, I'm just about to dish up, you guys keep talking."

"What did you say?" Kidd asked.

"I told him I was coming here, and he said maybe some other time, and then I left because it was so awkward!" She opened her bottle of cider and poured it into the glass. "Do I want to be dating someone? Probably. Do I want it to be Owen Campbell? Absolutely not!"

"What's wrong with DC Campbell?" Liz asked. It was a question that only someone who didn't work with DC Campbell would ask.

"He's just…"

"He's DC Campbell," Zoe finished. "But we're talking about work and that's boring. What were you talking about before I got here?"

Liz eyed Zoe gleefully, knowing that she would have someone on her side in this and Kidd felt his stomach drop.

"I'm trying to convince Ben to go to his school

reunion this week," Liz said. "He's saying he doesn't want to go but not giving a real reason, so…" Liz shrugged and gestured to the two of them. "Discuss." She went back to serving up dinner, Kidd sending daggers into the back of her head.

"Come on then," Zoe said, turning back to him, taking a victorious sip of her cider before she carried on speaking. "What's the reason you're not going?"

"I…I don't have the best memories of that school," Kidd said. "I think, as a night, it will be dull and I don't really want to use up a whole evening that I could be spending with Liz or you or John, hanging out with a bunch of people from my high school that I don't even talk to anymore."

Zoe eyed him carefully, seeming to process this for a moment. She eventually shrugged. "That's actually a pretty fair reason," she said. "All I'm saying, though, is that it could be fun. You could go with John, make an evening of it, just show off your life a little bit and go home. It might not be all that bad."

The phone started ringing, a shrill chime that seemed to rip through the whole kitchen. Liz called out an apology and said that she'd get it. Zoe's laser focus was still on Kidd.

"Thoughts?"

Kidd shrugged. "I don't know, that's not a bad idea."

"Really?"

"It might not be horrible if I go with someone," he said. "I mean, honestly, the worst part about going would be that I would be there by myself and it would be a terrible throwback to being fourteen and so awkward."

"What's the difference now?" Zoe said with a laugh.

"The difference now is that I'm awkward, but have a badge and a duty to pretend that I'm not."

Zoe lifted her glass to cheers him. "I will drink to that."

"To what?" Kidd asked. "Faking our way through our careers?"

Zoe nodded. "Exactly that."

They clinked their glasses together, the two of them taking long gulps from their drinks. Kidd had been working with Zoe for the past ten years or so. They'd been put on a team together and they just happened to click. Zoe didn't take any nonsense from anybody, and that included Kidd. Even though he was technically her boss, it didn't feel like that half the time. She'd put it best when he'd come back from leave a couple of weeks ago —they were friends first, colleagues second.

Liz reappeared in the kitchen, clutching the phone in her hand. She looked like she'd had the wind knocked out of her sails. Kidd's mind immediately went to the worst-case scenario, wondering who it could have been on the phone.

"That was Greg," Liz said. She looked up at them. She didn't have tears in her eyes, so maybe it wasn't all that bad, but she still looked pretty hurt by whatever had been said. "He's not coming home for dinner, apparently something at work came up."

Kidd let out a heavy breath. He'd expected worse than that.

"No problem," Kidd said. "We can save some food for him, it will be fine."

"Yeah," she said. "Sorry, we just argued about it. I've barely seen him for the past couple of weeks. Miss my husband, you know?"

Zoe put her glass down and hurried over to Liz, wrapping her in a hug. Kidd followed suit and did the same. He hated seeing his sister hurting. Greg was a good guy most of the time, Kidd didn't want to think the worst of him, but he certainly didn't want anyone making his sister feel like that.

Liz pulled herself out of the hug and took a deep breath.

"Okay," she said. "Wow, didn't expect to be almost crying tonight." She shook herself a little, fixing the smile back onto her face. "He's just working a lot, and it's obviously getting to me more than I thought. Whew. Okay. Let's get to the table or this is going to go cold. Ben, you want to grab the wine?"

Zoe took Liz into the dining room while Kidd headed back to the kitchen and grabbed the bottle of wine. He was unable to shake the feeling that something wasn't quite right. He shook it from his head, sure that he was overthinking it.

CHAPTER
THREE

Dinner was delicious. Once they'd sat down and started eating, it was as if the conversation Liz had with Greg never happened, something Kidd was certainly glad about. He didn't like seeing his younger sister upset.

They worked their way through the roast talking about the school reunion still. Kidd decided somewhere along the way that he would ask John if he wanted to go with him. Maybe it would be fun. But at least if it wasn't, he would be able to get out of there pretty swiftly.

They worked their way through the rest of the meal, Kidd and Zoe clearing up while Liz checked on the kids, the three of them drinking coffee and chatting until Liz could barely keep her eyes open.

"I'm sorry," she said through a yawn. "It's barely nine o'clock and I'm yawning like I've pulled a full shift."

"You have pulled a full shift," Kidd said. "Those kids are a handful."

"You're not wrong," Liz replied, downing the last of her coffee.

There was a sound from the front door, all three of them freezing and turning in the direction of the hallway. Someone struggled to get their keys in the door and then quickly opened it, shivering as they stepped inside. Greg was home.

They heard him kick his shoes off and head down the corridor towards the kitchen. When he turned into the dining room and saw them all sitting there, his face dropped a little. He'd obviously forgotten that tonight was happening, and Liz had decided not to remind him about it over the phone.

Greg was a fine-looking man, tall, broad-shouldered, his dark hair cropped close to his head, a little stubble around his jawline. He was in a shirt and a pair of smart trousers, his collar open, his tie hanging out of his pocket. Kidd knew that look. Someone who had been on shift all day and it had been so hard and tiring that you find yourself half undressed before you've even made it to the car. He looked absolutely beat. But there was something else, something in his face that Kidd couldn't quite place…

"Evening," he said, his voice a little gruff. "I didn't know we had company tonight."

"We planned it a couple of weeks ago," Liz said quietly. "Remember? Just a little dinner party with Ben and Zoe, this is Zoe, DS Sanchez, they work together in the Met."

Zoe said her hellos, Kidd waved from where he was sitting. You couldn't cut the tension in the room with a knife, you'd need something a heck of a lot sharper. A saw perhaps. Liz wasn't happy, that much Kidd could see and he didn't want to get in the way of anything.

"Well," Kidd said, standing from the table. "It's getting late."

"Yeah," Zoe said, quickly following his lead. "We've got to be in the office early tomorrow. Thanks so much for dinner, Liz."

Liz looked up and plastered a smile on her face, but Kidd could tell that she was playing the happy housewife. That Greg coming home had put a damper on what had been a very lovely evening.

"Thank you so much for coming," she said. "We'll have to do it again sometime."

They said their goodbyes, Kidd promising that he'd be in touch with Liz later on in the week to check-in, Zoe promising they won't leave it so long next time, and then they were out in the cold.

Kidd wrapped his coat around himself, shoving his hands deep into the pockets. It was glacial. It was February, and it felt like this winter had gone on forever. If there was one thing Benjamin Kidd hated, it was the cold.

"That was uncomfortable," Zoe said as they walked towards her car. "Very uncomfortable."

Kidd nodded. "They're obviously going through

some stuff," he said. "I think we did the right thing by getting out of there."

"I'll say," Zoe said. "So, I didn't get a chance to ask, we managed to avoid the topic for the whole of dinner. How are things with you and John?"

"Me and John?"

"Yes, Ben, you and John," Zoe said. "Don't repeat things back at me to save time. What the heck is that?"

Kidd laughed as they walked. "Things are good," he said. "It's early days and we're not about to go booking a venue, but it's nice. I'm happy." He checked his phone. "He was at the Druid's Head tonight with some friends. I might see if he's still around."

Zoe widened her eyes at him. "Detective Inspector Benjamin Kidd staying out late on a school night," she said. "People will talk."

"And I expect you to shut them up."

"Sure thing, boss," she said with a wink. "It's good to see you happy and before you say that you were happy before." She'd obviously seen Kidd opening his mouth to retort. "I know you were, but now I'm seeing you happier and it's nice."

"Thanks," Kidd said.

He walked Zoe to her car, bidding her goodnight before he started walking towards the middle of town and the Druid's Head, the usual haunt for the team at Kingston Police Station. He wouldn't stay for long, maybe stopping for one before heading home. He didn't want to get in the way of John's night.

He got there in pretty good time, making his way to

the front door to see John was stood in the window, laughing with a few of his friends. He was wearing a blue checked shirt, his hair, usually in a perfectly placed quiff had fallen a little bit forward, but he brushed it out of his face, still grinning at whatever had just been said.

He looked like he was having a good time. A good enough time that Ben decided that maybe he would leave it for tonight and talk to him tomorrow. That was, until John saw him through the window. He smiled and beckoned Kidd inside. He shook his head.

John made his way outside, not bothering to grab his jacket so the second he stepped into the cold, his hands made their way under his armpits for warmth. He tottered over to Kidd, all smiles, eyes sparkling even though it was dark. How did he do that?

"I was hoping I'd see you," John said, still smiling.

"Were you?" Kidd replied. "That's...that's nice. I'm glad I came then."

"Are you coming in? As much as I'm enjoying standing out here talking to you, I'm freezing," he said. "You can meet the gang if you want?"

"The gang?" Kidd replied. "You sure you're ready for me to meet the gang."

John shrugged. "If you want to."

Kidd smiled and looked back at the window at the people who were now staring out at him, the guy who'd dragged their friend away. He instantly felt guilty.

"I actually came to invite you out tomorrow night," Kidd said, stuffing his fingers down into his pockets, trying to ignore the sweat on his palms. "I've got a school reunion that I don't want to go to, and I thought maybe we could go together. Well, it was DS Sanchez's suggestion, she thought..." he trailed off. "And I agreed that..." He shook his head. "Do you want to come?"

John was still smiling. He looked like a slightly more frozen version of the John McAdams that Kidd was enjoying getting to know, but he still looked incredibly handsome when he smiled. And that smile was all for Ben.

"Sure thing," he replied. "Lunch *and* an embarrassingly cringe school reunion, I am blessed."

"You don't have to if you don't—"

"I'm coming," he said. "Now are you coming back inside with me?"

Kidd looked around John again, the people in the window quickly readjusting themselves to go back to whatever it was they were now fake-talking about. He tried not to laugh.

"I'll leave you to it," Kidd said. "I'll see you tomorrow for lunch, yeah?"

"I'm working from home so I can take lunch pretty much whenever," John replied. "So just let me know."

They stood there for a few seconds, a strange amount of distance between them that John eventually closed, planting a kiss on Ben's cheek.

"See you tomorrow," he said quietly before turning back to the Druid's and walking inside.

Not wanting to see the reaction of his friends when John made it back to the table, DI Benjamin Kidd quickly walked away, starting back towards his house.

He made his way out of Kingston's Market Square, taking a shortcut down to the riverside. It was the long way around to get home, sure, but he wanted the walk to take in the night. It may have been glacial, but this was his favourite spot in the whole town, and even though there were the sounds of restaurants in the background, happy couples walking by, groups of friends heading out for drinks, he liked it here.

His phone buzzed in his pocket and he took it out, seeing he had a couple of missed calls from DCI Weaver and a message from John. He went to that first.

> Hope you had a lovely evening, was nice to see you, however briefly. I'm looking forward to lunch tomorrow. And the reunion. Xx

> Nice to see you too. One o'clock suit you? Xx

The message came back through almost immediately, which made Kidd smile.

> Perfect. I'll see you then. Sleep tight. Xx

> You too xx

Kidd found himself hesitating before listening to the messages from DCI Weaver. He was off duty now. He was trying to get better at the whole work-life balance thing, learning to switch off so he didn't end up staying up half the night thinking about it.

He'd been terrible at that before he ended up getting

signed off with stress. But Weaver wouldn't call unless it was urgent. It was almost like a change in the air around him. Something had happened, and he'd called Kidd because why? Because he needed someone to talk it over with? If he listened, he knew he wouldn't sleep tonight.

Before he could stop himself, he moved to switch off his phone when another message came through. One from a name he hadn't seen in a very long time.

Andrea Peyton.

BUY JUST KEEP BREATHING NOW

ACKNOWLEDGMENTS

The first people I need to thank are those in the group who have helped to make this possible. This wouldn't have happened without you and I cannot thank you enough for the support, insight and encouragement. Bill, in particular, thank you for pushing me to do this.

Thank you so much to my wonderful editor Hanna for all of your useful edits and to Meg for this gorgeous cover, I am so so thrilled with it and I am so excited to be working with you on it.

To my marvellous partner, JW who backed me on this so heavily. Thank you, thank you, thank you.

And to all of you who have read this far, thank you for your support. If you enjoyed it, please feel free to drop a review on Amazon and let people know that you liked it, it really helps us out. And hopefully I will see you for the next one. Until then…

GS x

ABOUT THE AUTHOR

GS Rhodes has been writing for as long as he can remember, scribbling stories on spare bits of paper and hoping to one day share those stories with the world. The DI Benjamin Kidd series is GS Rhodes first foray into crime writing, combining a love of where he has lived for a lot of his life with his love of a good mystery. Now well into this series, he is also writing a spin-off featuring DS Zoe Sanchez in the starring role, starting with Deadly Tears.

 facebook.com/Gsrhodesauthor

 twitter.com/gs_rhodes

 instagram.com/gs_rhodes

Printed in Great Britain
by Amazon

37472087R00189